Jack Vance

The View from Chickweed's Window

Jack Vance

The View from Chickweed's Window

John H Vance

Spatterlight
P R E S S
340 S. Lemon Ave #1916
Walnut, CA 91789

www.jackvance.com

Jack Vance

The View from
Chickweed's Window

Chapter I

In the year 1907 a curious adventure befell Harry Botham, partner in the firm Botham and Brewer, Commercial Factors of Shanghai.

Returning early from a party Botham surprised a trio of robbers in the act of looting his house. His small daughter Flora lay trussed and gagged as a preliminary to kidnapping; the *amah* huddled on the floor moaning. By the wall stood the house-boy, a dagger pinning his ear to the woodwork.

Botham surveyed the scene from the darkness of the hall. Quietly he took a cavalry saber from the wall and charged. The most stalwart of the bandits he cut down with a single blow; the second, a stripling of fourteen, scrambled like a monkey up the front of a cabinet, which toppled, spilling Botham's porcelains and pinning the youth to the floor. The third threw himself at Botham's feet.

Panting, Botham surveyed the scene. His porcelain lay in shards; the air reeked with blood and the stink of fright. Ting the house-boy pulled the dagger from his ear, and darting forward began to hack at the now-passive bandit. Botham stopped him. "Go for the police. Let them deal with the situation."

"My lord," came the voice of the bandit, "show us mercy."

"Mercy, ha!" rasped Botham. "My porcelain: destroyed! My daughter: out of her mind with terror!" The *amah* now began to release Flora from her bonds.

"We are victims of an evil destiny," said the bandit, "as witness the outcome of this night's work. The police will torture us, myself and my son, indiscriminately: this is their habit. Your beneficial grasp controls the future course of our lives."

"Torture is no more than you deserve," declared Botham. "Ting, go fetch the —"

"My lord, I implore your attention," said the bandit. "Your daughter will soon forget her alarm. As for the porcelain — I speak now with the absolute candor of a man in despair — the quality was so deficient that I had intended not even to steal it. You have been victimized by unscrupulous merchants. Your loss is not only of small compass, but may well be susceptible to repair."

A nuance of tone engaged Botham's interest. "You have a collection of your own?"

"I am an ordinary robber; such an ambition exceeds my dreams. Nevertheless, at some risk, I can procure for you a pair of inordinately beautiful vases, objects of great age and value. These should not only assuage your indignation, but perhaps will induce you to allow myself and my son our liberty."

"Where are these vases?" inquired Botham. "To whom do they belong?"

"The details are inconsequential. When I place the objects before you, by any practical test they may be regarded as my personal property."

There was further discussion; in the end the bandit was allowed to go off to fetch the vases, while the son remained as a hostage. The wounded man, with the house-boy's help, bandaged himself with a rag and sat slumped in a daze.

Within an hour the bandit returned, eyes glittering with excitement. He carried an object wrapped in newspaper. Botham received him alone in the study, and, removing the newspaper, discovered a single vase, something over a foot high, the glaze a smoky mauve glimmer of a richness beyond Botham's experience. Reverently examining the vase he found on the foot the mark *Hai-lun-tse*, and realized that he held one of the most precious relics of the Sung Dynasty. Pitching his voice in a casual tone he said, "This is certainly an interesting piece, almost the equal to one or two of my own, now unfortunately destroyed. You spoke of two vases. Where is the other?"

"I am fortunate to have succeeded so well," said the bandit. "Conditions were more rigorous than I had expected, and it was a choice between the one or none at all."

"Very well," said Botham, "I see you have done your best. Be off then, and never let me see your face again. Unless, of course, you choose to part with further pieces from your collection, which I shall be glad to examine. Especially the mate to this particular vase."

"I understand you perfectly," declared the bandit. "May the future deal fruitfully with us both."

The following day Botham learned of the self-inflicted death of Baron Iso Matsukoku, Chief of the Japanese Foreign Trade Commission. According to the Shanghai *Daily Express* Baron Matsukoku had been entrusted with a ceremonial gift to Emperor Meiji from the Dragon Empress herself: a pair of priceless Sung vases, glazed a unique mauve celadon. One of the vases had disappeared during the night and Baron Matsukoku had manifested his humiliation in the traditional manner.

Botham crated the vase, locked it in a trunk, and gave up all hope of acquiring its mate.

There was still a further aftermath of the affair. During the conflict Botham had suffered a cut across the back of his hand, which became seriously infected. At the hospital he was tended by a fresh-faced nurse newly arrived from England. Her name was Mary Higgins, and Harry Botham, a widower, proposed marriage as soon as he was discharged from the hospital. Mary Higgins accepted, they were married, and in the year 1909 became parents to a chubby blonde daughter named Ruth.

Botham and Brewer prospered; Flora and Ruth Botham grew through childhood, adolescence, and each in turn reigned as belle of the International Settlement. Flora, seven years older than Ruth, was tall and dark, with exquisite features and an elegant manner. In 1926, at the most fashionable wedding of the season, she married Maurice Brewer, son of Harry Botham's partner.

For a wedding present Harry Botham gave the couple a trip around the world. In 1932 a son Kendall was born and in 1935 a second son Oliver.

Ruth Botham was almost the antithesis to her half-sister. She was blonde, slight, round and soft as a kitten. Flora was inclined to peremptoriness; Ruth coaxed. Flora's clothes were immaculate; she bathed twice, occasionally three times a day, and never became accustomed to the smells drifting in from Soochow Creek, or the wretched human clottings of Greater Shanghai beyond the confines of the Settlement. Ruth accepted life more or less as it came, laughed easily and made friends with persons Flora considered unsuitable. One of these friends was Kenneth Enright, a young Methodist missionary stationed in Japan. Ruth fell in love with Kenneth despite Flora's disapproval. Kenneth Enright not only lacked wealth and *savoir-faire*; he was also an American. Ruth laughed at Flora's objections and in 1929 made Kenneth ludicrously happy by marrying him.

Harry Botham, despite Flora's appeals, had remained neutral, remarking that since Ruth must live with her husband she should certainly be allowed the privilege of selecting him. Flora never became reconciled to the match, and snubbed poor Kenneth elaborately.

On the day before the wedding Harry Botham took Kenneth and Ruth aside and revealed that he was planning to send them around the world as he had Flora and Maurice. Stammering with embarrassment, Kenneth stated that while he appreciated the offer he could not possibly take so much time from his work. Ruth amplified Kenneth's remarks by explaining that it simply didn't *look* right for a missionary to indulge himself in conspicuous luxury while children of his parish suffered from malnutrition. She added saucily that if her father so chose he could donate the value of the trip to the Japanese Methodist Church, but this Harry Botham refused to do. He liked Kenneth personally, but he harbored the gravest doubts as to the ultimate value of his work. Why foist the beliefs of an obscure Arabian tribe upon a people with highly developed traditions of their own?

Kenneth replied mildly that Mr. Botham's opinions of course were to be respected, which amused Harry Botham. He clapped Kenneth jauntily upon the back. Ruth eyed her father with suspicion. "Very well then," said Botham, "in that case, you shall have one of my most prized possessions: a vase seven hundred years old, certainly one of the most beautiful in existence."

"Papa!" exclaimed Ruth in consternation. She as well as Flora knew something of the history of the vase.

"Yes, my dear?"

"Do you consider the vase — a suitable present?"

"Certainly. Why not?"

Kenneth looked from Ruth to Botham in puzzlement, but held his curiosity in check. Ruth shrugged and said no more. Flora, learning of the gift, was furious with disappointment. She long had coveted the fabulous vase; to see it bestowed upon her sister exasperated her beyond measure.

Kenneth and Ruth returned to Japan with the vase packed casually in their luggage. They set up housekeeping in the quaint old rectory at Onomichi overlooking the Inland Sea, the vase on display in their *tokonoma*.

The years passed: for Kenneth and Ruth happy years. On the continent were mutterings of war, presages of terrible times ahead.

Mary Botham died suddenly in 1930, apparently from food poisoning; Harry Botham survived her only two years and died on Easter Sunday, 1932 at the age of 60. His estate passed in equal shares to Flora and Ruth.

At the funeral Flora mentioned the Sung vase. "Do you know what Daddy's last words to me were?"

"I'm sure I don't," said Ruth drily.

"He spoke of the vase. He told me — speaking ever so huskily, for he could hardly breathe — he told me, 'Flora, dearest, the Sung vase is on my conscience.'"

"As I can well believe."

Flora ignored the interruption. "He said, 'I intended that vase for you and Maurice; you two will enjoy it ever so much more than Ruth and her husband.' Mind you," Flora emphasized, "these were his last words: 'Ask her for the vase, explain that I made a mistake; Ruth is generous; she will understand.'"

"I understand only too well," said Ruth. "My answer is 'no'."

"Ruth! You refuse to honor Father's last words?"

"He seems to have been delirious."

"Ruth! How can you speak so!"

Ruth patted Flora's arm. "Please, Flora, dear — do let's be sensible. You've wanted that vase since Father made us the gift. But you can't have it. Understand? So let's just forget the matter once and for all."

Flora swept off in an angry rustle of black silk crêpe.

Ruth turned back to Kenneth, who stood apart from the discussion. "My sister," said Ruth, "is an extraordinary woman. As the years go by it almost appears that she is becoming — shall we say? — covetous."

Kenneth made a noncommittal sound. "Just a mannerism, surely."

"Kenneth," snapped Ruth, "sometimes you are absolutely maddening."

"My dear," protested Kenneth, "what have I done?"

"I realize that your profession doesn't allow you the normal scope for slander and back-biting. But Kenneth, for mercy's sake, please realize that there is such a thing as simple, ordinary meanness."

"I'd be the last to deny it," declared Kenneth. "Nevertheless, I feel that the treatment a person receives is only a reflection of his own conduct."

Ruth sighed. "Let's go in for a cup of tea."

Returning to Japan they discussed their newly inherited wealth. "I'll make no suggestions, of course," said Kenneth, wistfully. "The income is yours to spend as you like."

"Well," said Ruth, "for one thing we shall both have new clothes. Standing beside Flora I felt positively dowdy. And you, Kenny, I can really see my face in your coat."

"Yes, such an expenditure might well be in order."

Ruth continued briskly: "And I think that now we can afford to start our family." Kenneth mumbled something about pregnancy being a terrible nuisance. Ruth agreed. "Then we'll save a certain amount of money — a good deal — to make sure our children have a decent start in life."

"Yes, to be sure."

"And then," Ruth hugged Kenneth's arm, "the rest goes to you, and there should be a great deal. And you can carry through all your wonderful ideas and projects."

But Kenneth did not react quite as happily as Ruth had expected. "What's wrong?" asked Ruth. "Aren't you pleased?"

"Under normal circumstances I'd be more than happy," said Kenneth.

"These aren't normal circumstances?"

"Lately I've become ever more uncertain as to what the future holds. The news is often disquieting…"

"Kenneth, stop," Ruth laughed nervously. "You'll give me a real case of shudders."

Back in Onomichi the Enrights resumed their old lives, hoping now for children. In 1933 Ruth became pregnant and miscarried. In 1935 she bore a child which lived only three hours.

About this time the Enrights received a letter from Maurice Brewer, announcing the birth of his second son, who would be christened Oliver. He likewise wrote of plans to sell his own and Flora's holdings in the firm Botham and Brewer, comprising a 75% interest. He had interested a buyer who would also take the Enrights' 25% should they also choose to sell. While the price offered was substantial, it in no way reflected the true worth of the company. The buyer, indeed, was getting a bargain. "However," wrote Maurice, "these are not reassuring times and the financial climate is very uncertain. Flora and I have decided to live — at least for a time — in San Francisco. I don't wish to influence unduly your future plans, but we all realize the very unsettled conditions here and in Europe. I feel that the wise course is to sell out and invest elsewhere."

"Well, well," said Ruth. "So the Brewers are clearing out."

Kenneth smeared marmalade on his toast — they were eating breakfast under the pines of the rectory garden. "From their standpoint, very wisely."

Ruth studied the letter. "5,000 pounds we're offered. For an income of eight hundred a year. Scarcely a generous offer."

"We must consider current conditions," said Kenneth. "As Maurice points out, the atmosphere is going from bad to worse."

Ruth leaned back and studied Kenneth. "You think we should sell?" she inquired at last.

"Yes," said Kenneth. In a facetious voice he added, "For the sake of our unborn child. Five thousand pounds will provide him, or her, or them, a very pleasant nest-egg. And if we lose our principal — there'll be nothing."

"Very well," said Ruth. "I'll write Maurice and tell him to sell. For the sake of our unborn child. If any."

"We shall not despair."

In due course a check for 5,000 pounds arrived, and the Enrights immediately invested in United States Postal Savings Bonds.

Full-scale war inundated China. In Europe Hitler marched into Austria, Czechoslovakia, and presently Poland, but the quiet life of the Methodist Church at Onomichi went on as before.

In 1939 Ruth became pregnant a third time, and in April of 1940 she bore a girl whom she named Luellen.

On December 7, 1941, the world changed dramatically for the Enrights. The church was closed; the Enrights were interned.

Conditions in the camp were extremely harsh, the Japanese revealing a strange new aspect to their complicated personalities.

In 1944 Ruth died of malnutrition complicated by pneumonia, and the sunlight forever vanished from Kenneth's life. Only the need to care for his daughter gave him the will to exist.

In 1945 the war ended; the world changed dramatically once again, and again the Japanese became polite. With nowhere else to go, Kenneth and Luellen returned to Onomichi. Although the memories surrounding the rectory were almost more than he could bear, he reopened the church, and tried to resume his old life.

There was no longer a challenge to his work, no zest, no fulfillment. Only the deadening knowledge of failure, defeat, of wasted years and spent dreams, with youth and joy and his loving wife forever gone.

CHAPTER II

ON THE MORNING OF April 28, 1948 the *SS President Madison* arrived at San Francisco from the Far East. The sun had only just risen as the ship slid under the Golden Gate Bridge; the city stood on its hills cool and white, every architectural detail sharply defined through the clear air.

In a house on Pacific Heights Maurice Brewer had already arisen and dressed himself in a suit of heavy gray tweed. Standing by the window of the upstairs sitting-room he watched the *President Madison* slide along the curve of the Embarcadero. He glanced at his watch, turned and went down the hall to the door of Flora's bedroom. He rapped, listened, then rapped again. "Flora! Are you coming along? Or aren't you? It's quite late."

There was no answer. Maurice rapped again. "Flora!"

From within came Flora's voice, contriving somehow to convey irritation and a rather maddening degree of self-possession in the same tone. "There's no enormous hurry, Maurice, not in the least."

"The ship docks at any minute!" called Maurice through the door, but Flora made no further response.

Maurice turned away muttering. "Confound it, woman, you'll be late for your own funeral." He went back to the window. The *President Madison* was drifting at slow speed almost out of sight past the Ferry Building; as Maurice watched a pair of tugs churned alongside. He turned once again toward the hall, then thought better of it, and clenching his teeth thrust his hands in his pockets and waited. Maurice Brewer, now 52, was a big man, burly rather than fat, with a round pink-cheeked face, a short nose, wild-boar eyes with bristling eyebrows. He had a tonsure of dry-looking chestnut-gray hair, and heavy lips which he held compressed as he waited for Flora. His expression was sullen and peevish; when ten minutes later Flora appeared, wearing a gray suit, a lavender-gray coat with fox collar, he made no comment, but only turned toward the stairs.

On the first floor Flora turned aside toward the dining room; Maurice paused, stared after her. "Now where are you going?"

"I must speak to Benjamin about changing the furniture."

"'Changing the furniture'? What furniture?"

"In the bedroom, of course." She disappeared into the kitchen, while Maurice stood fuming by the door. Minutes passed, and presently Flora appeared. Maurice pointed to his wristwatch. "Do you realize what time it is? The ship's sure to be docked."

Flora's response was the merest suggestion of an airy sniff. Sweeping past Maurice, she went down the entry walk drawing on her gloves. Leisurely she inspected their car, a big black Lincoln only a few months old. A bird had voided upon the hood and Flora sped forward to examine the spot. She turned back toward the house. "Now where are you going?" cried Maurice.

"I told Benjamin to wipe down the car very carefully," said Flora over her shoulder. "Obviously he's neglected his work."

"That was yesterday!" Maurice called after her. "And we haven't time —"

Benjamin, the Filipino house-boy, was duly summoned, and ordered to clean the car. While Maurice stood first on one foot then the other Benjamin fetched a damp rag and wiped away the spot.

Maurice started the engine, and they sped away down the street. "Please, Maurice," said Flora, "drive carefully. You're taking quite unnecessary risks."

"Do we want to meet this ship or don't we?" asked Maurice between clenched teeth. "Sometimes I can't understand you! Fooling and fiddling around for an hour now. It's not as if we were meeting an adult or someone who knew what to do."

"I'm sure she'll be quite all right," said Flora, looking squarely ahead. "And after all..." She left the sentence significantly unfinished.

"And what's all this about Benjamin moving furniture?" demanded Maurice. "What furniture where?"

"I told Benjamin to bring up the nursery furniture, and put away the good rosewood."

Maurice stared. "What in heaven's name…"

"We really know nothing about this girl. She may be careless or destructive, and the rosewood chiffonier is too valuable to risk."

Maurice snorted. "What a pack of nonsense!"

Flora's lips trembled in a wintry unfathomable smile, and Maurice said no more. He swung out Lombard Street to the Embarcadero, and proceeded to Pier 37, far to the south of Market Street.

"The ship's already docked," said Maurice grimly. "I must say, this is a poor way to meet someone. Especially a child."

"We're arriving in plenty of time," Flora said unconcernedly. "And after all, this responsibility is one we've never solicited."

Maurice glanced sidelong at his wife, shrugged. "If that's how you feel, there's certainly no reason for me to worry." He nosed the Lincoln into a parking place, opened the door for Flora, and together they entered the pier.

The gangplank had been secured; debarking passengers were passing behind the trestles erected by customs. Maurice sought through the shifting groups. "About all we know of the girl is that she's eight years old and blonde…"

Flora pointed a gloved finger to a plump urchin with fat cheeks and yellow hair cut in a Dutch-boy bob. "Perhaps that is Luellen. Her mother was inclined to sturdiness."

"Too young," said Maurice. "And Ruth wasn't sturdy; what a word!… No more than nicely filled out."

Flora said no more, but shivered her shoulders. "It's icy in here; these people should take more care."

Maurice paid her no heed. He pulled out his pipe, and searching through the crowd, charged it with tobacco. Suddenly he pointed. "There she is, I'm certain."

Flora turned her head. By the far wall stood an elderly couple in dark clothes, both tall, gaunt and patently respectable. By their side, very quietly, stood a slight, rather pale girl with blonde hair in a pair of braids.

"Missionaries," said Flora, voice almost imperceptibly tinged with deprecation. Maurice, married to Flora now for twenty-two years, had developed so sensitive an ear that even the quality of Flora's silences conveyed meanings. In the matter of missionaries, however, their attitudes matched so closely that he was barely conscious that she had spoken. "I'll inquire."

He strode through the crowd, leaving Flora standing alone. A porter, staggering under the weight of two suitcases, brushed close, vexing her further. "Well!" she said frostily. Turning, she walked after Maurice, who already had engaged the elderly couple in conversation.

The girl watched her approach. Her face was very calm, thought Flora. A self-possessed child, probably willful. There was no obvious resemblance either to Kenneth or to Ruth in the round young face.

"Ah, here is my wife," said Maurice in his bluffest, most genial manner. "Flora, the Reverend and Mrs. Murtries from Shihara. And this is little Luellen. The Murtries have been kind enough to take her under their wing."

"No trouble whatever," declared the Reverend Murtries. He stood six feet two, thin as an eel in his rusty black suit. "Lulu is a very sensible young lady."

His wife said in a voice of diffuse complaint, "We were wondering what we would do when no one came to meet the child."

"An unavoidable delay," explained Maurice. "Unfortunate, but we finally arrived. All's well that ends well. Right?"

"Yes, indeed," said Murtries, without conviction. He looked at his wife, stooped, picked up his old straw valise. "Very well, since Lulu is in good hands, we must be on our way. Our train leaves in two hours."

"We're traveling straight through to Idaho," explained Mrs. Murtries.

The Reverend Murtries patted Lulu's sleek blonde head. "Goodby, little lady, be a good girl and write to us."

"Yes, Mr. Murtries," said Lulu. "Goodby." She held out her hand, and Mrs. Murtries gave it a quick twitch. "Goodby, Lulu." She spoke above Lulu's head to Flora, "Such a bright child, but she's had to grow up ten years ahead of time. Wartime conditions, you understand."

"I'm afraid I don't understand," said Flora.

"My dear, you've never lived in the East," said Mrs. Murtries.

Maurice laughed politely. "To the contrary, Mrs. Murtries. We're old China hands, lived in Shanghai many years, both of us."

"Indeed," said Mrs. Murtries vaguely. "Well, well. As much as we'd love a good gossip, I'm afraid we must be on our way." Bowing and nodding the Murtries took their leave.

Maurice looked down to Lulu, patted her gingerly on the shoulder. "Now, finally we can get acquainted. I'm your Uncle Maurice and this is your Aunt Flora."

"How do you do," said Flora.

"They call you Lulu, do they?" Maurice asked jovially.

"Yes. But my real name is Luellen."

"I see. Well, we're very glad to have you come live with us. We've got two nice boys — a bit older than you — but I'm sure you'll get along beautifully."

Lulu nodded. She hesitated, then twisted her face into a frown of concentration. "My father didn't tell me when I'd be going home again. Did he tell you?"

Maurice looked off across the cavernous interior of the pier, raising his bushy eyebrows at the difficulty of the situation.

In a voice clear and quiet Flora said, "Your father is very ill, and you'll be staying with us for a long time."

Lulu's face went very still. "Is he dead?"

Flora gave her shoulders a little shake. "It's just as well that you find out now. He is dead, yes."

Lulu's eyes glistened. She turned her head away and looked blindly out toward the street.

"We're very sorry," said Maurice. "And after awhile you'll be happy in your new home." He swung his arms briskly. "But now, we must see to your luggage."

Lulu handed him a yellow claim check. "This is for my trunk. And I have a suitcase."

"Attend to the luggage, Maurice," said Flora. "Luellen and I will wait in the car. And be exceedingly careful...You know what I mean." She extended her hand to Lulu. "We'll have our first little private conversation."

Maurice took the claim checks and Flora shepherded Lulu to the car. They climbed into the rear seat. Flora leaned back into the corner, surveyed Lulu through half-closed eyes. "Did you have a nice trip over?" she asked.

"Yes, very nice. Except about my daddy. I knew he was sick, I knew he was sending me away..."

"Now, now, let's not cry. Crying never helps anything."

Lulu's mouth twisted and strained; tears glistened on her cheeks. "But I'll never see him again."

"Today," said Flora, "we'll take you downtown and buy you some new clothes. I suppose you need absolutely everything."

Lulu rubbed at her eyes with her wrist. "I have lots of clothes," she said in a dreary voice.

"But you want to look nice, don't you? At our house all of us try to look as pretty and clean and well-groomed as we can."

Lulu nodded without enthusiasm.

"Then we'll have to think about school. Let me see, you're eight years old, I believe?"

"Yesterday was my birthday," said Lulu. "I was eight yesterday."

"And what grade are you in? Or did you go to school in Japan?"

"I went to the Missionary School at Onomichi, and I was in the third grade."

"I see. Well, for the rest of the term you shall attend Pacific Heights Grade School, where Kendall and Oliver both went." She ran her eyes critically over Lulu's black wool jumper, the knee-high black stockings, the white blouse. "Yes, we must buy some new clothes at once. You're part of the Brewer family now, and we're very careful of our appearance."

Lulu nodded. "All right, Aunt Flora."

Maurice returned with Lulu's black fibre suitcase, which he tucked into the back. Flora looked sharply at Maurice. "Where is the trunk?"

"I'm having it delivered to the house," said Maurice.

"No," said Flora incisively. "You know how the moving men are. Have them bring the trunk here, very carefully, and we'll load it into the car."

Maurice stared at her with narrowed eyes. "That is utterly ridiculous. I'll do no such thing!"

"We are not going to move from here without that trunk." Flora's voice was sibilant and soft. Lulu made herself as small as possible in the seat.

Maurice straightened up, so that they could no longer see his face through the automobile window.

"Please hurry, Maurice," said Flora. "This isn't the nicest of districts to be waiting in."

From Maurice's unseen face came a snort of disgust, but he turned and marched back into the pier structure.

Flora sat in silence, face turned away from Lulu, who stared unseeingly at her knees, bare between the tops of her black stockings and the hem of her black skirt.

Maurice returned with a porter who wheeled the trunk on a dolly. To the accompaniment of Maurice's muttered cursing, the trunk was wedged into the luggage compartment and made fast with bits of old manila rope.

Maurice hulked himself into the front seat, settled with an ill-natured grunt. "We look like a family of farm-workers...Ridiculous, hauling luggage...A hundred movers in the city."

"Please let's be going, Maurice. I have a great deal to do today."

"I have no intention whatever of remaining here," said Maurice. He started the engine, swung across the Embarcadero, and headed back toward the house on Belvedere Street.

Chapter III

Lulu had never known a city like this. Tokyo was flat, drab, ramshackle, dreary, and miserable, as were Kobe, Osaka and Nagoya. Around her now rose white buildings taller than any she had ever seen, with windows flashing in the sun. Impressions crowded upon her too fast for assimilation, even had she felt eager and alert; but she looked unseeingly through the window, conscious only of a dark emptiness inside herself, which overflowed to contain all the universe. She thought of her father and the never-to-be-known-again rectory; her eyes moistened, tears ran down her cheeks.

Flora surveyed her without expression. "Come, Luellen," she said after a moment, "Crying won't help matters. All of us have troubles; what would you think if everyone cried?"

Maurice threw a glance over his shoulder, started to speak, then returned wordlessly to his driving. After a moment Flora shrugged slightly, turned and settled her fox around her neck. Lulu looked up through tear-blurred eyes at the backs of the two heads. Stealthily she drew a deep breath, blinked. In Flora's last cool inspection she had felt something she could not understand; it was almost as if Flora were glad she were crying. Without conscious volition Lulu wiped her eyes with her wrist and froze her face into a tight little mask. She drew another deep breath, resolutely turned to look out the window. They were passing through a hillside district of handsome old houses, two, three, or four stories high, depending on the slope. Maurice made two turns, drove up a very steep hill, and into a wide quiet street.

Maurice coasted to a halt, turned off the motor. With brassy cheerfulness he called, "Hoopla! We're home! Everybody out!"

Lulu fumbled with the door handle, let herself out upon the sidewalk; then reaching back in tugged her suitcase out after her.

They were parked in the middle of the block, in front of a tall multi-gabled house with a façade of tan stucco and dark half-timbering. The windows were divided into numerous small panes, and before each hung a window box flowing over with bright green and red geraniums. A brick walk led through the front lawn to a brick-paved vestibule. Lulu thought the house quite the grandest she had ever seen.

Maurice and Flora joined her on the sidewalk. "There you are," said Maurice. "Your new home. Little Miss Lulu Enright of 2413 Belvedere Street. Like it?"

Lulu nodded. "It's very nice."

Maurice picked up Lulu's suitcase. "Exactly what the place needed — a pretty young lady living in it."

Flora seemed to grimace. She turned and marched up the walk.

Maurice unlocked the door; they entered a large oak-paneled entry hall. Against the far wall stood a tall camphorwood cabinet displaying a three-foot bronze Buddha, a pair of blue Manchu petal-jars, a dragon carved from white jade. On the newel-post stood a gilded Bodhisattva, contemplating an incense brazier which exhaled a wisp of smoke. "You'd better help Benjamin with the trunk," Flora told Maurice. "Just take it up to the second floor. I'll show Luellen to her room." She crooked a finger. "Come along. Can you manage your suitcase?"

"Yes."

"Come along then." Flora started up the stairs, and Lulu followed, the suitcase bumping her legs.

At the second floor Flora turned down the hall, opened a door, waited for the now-panting Lulu. "This will be your room," said Flora. "There is —" She stopped short, looking into the room. Then she swept to the head of the stairs. "Maurice!" she called. "Send Benjamin here."

Maurice himself came up the stairs. "Benjamin is no longer here. He quit this morning."

Flora did not seem to hear. "I distinctly told him to bring up the oak nursery furniture, and take down the rosewood set!"

"That's why he quit," said Maurice drily. "He told Margaret there was too much work around here for one man."

"Bah!" snapped Flora. "Utter bosh!" Her nostrils had become white and pinched, her eyes glittered. Lulu watched aghast, the feeling of helplessness and despair heavier than ever. Oh, to be back at Onomichi!

Flora was speaking to Maurice. "You'll have to get help with the trunk. Go next door and ask Mrs. Hale to lend you Albert. He's always willing and pleasant; I don't see why we can't find a boy like Albert."

Maurice scowled. He looks like a big red-faced baby, thought Lulu. "I don't particularly care to bother Mrs. Hale," said Maurice. "After all —"

"We must get the trunk in the house, that's all there is to it," said Flora crisply. "And you can't manage by yourself."

Maurice wordlessly turned and went back down the stairs.

Flora went into the bedroom and looked around. Lulu timorously followed, dragging the suitcase.

"I had planned different furniture in here," said Flora. "There's a fine old suite that the boys used when they were your age. This is very valuable rosewood. But for now we'll use what's here. We must be careful — *very* careful indeed — of the furniture. No scratches, no dirty hands, no greasy clothes hanging over this fine wood, or on the upholstery."

"I don't have dirty hands," said Lulu, "and my clothes aren't greasy."

Flora had a trick of turning her head a trifle sidewise, looking down her nose, pursing her mouth into a small cold half-smile: an expression conveying skepticism, disbelief, the asseveration of superior understanding and knowledge. Ignoring Lulu's remark, she pointed. "You may use that bureau and that closet. All of us in this house are clean and neat; we put our shoes away and hang up our clothes." She turned and inspected Lulu carefully. "Do you wet the bed?"

Lulu blinked and her jaw dropped at the monstrous imputation. Her face burned. She could hardly find words. "No," she stammered. "No."

Flora nodded. "Your soiled clothes must be dropped at once down the chute; otherwise a room becomes stale. Come, I'll show you the chute."

She took Lulu along the hall, demonstrated the operation of the hinged door. "Now," said Flora, opening another door, "this is the lavatory, which you will use. For your baths you will have to share the bathroom upstairs with Kendall and Oliver. Temporarily, at any rate."

She swept down the hall and into the back sitting-room. Lulu followed slowly. Flora stopped by the rear window. Below was the back garden, terminated by a tall fence, and in the distance the gray-blue bay, bright in the sunshine. Flora motioned to Lulu. "Sit down, we'll have our little chat."

Lulu obediently settled into an armchair beside the fireplace.

"I realize," said Flora, "that living here will be different from your old life in Japan. *Much* different. You see, I knew your father and mother very well. Their way of doing things was probably quite suitable for the Japanese countryside and other missionaries, but here we live a different life altogether. I'm sure you'll be able to adjust." Looking down into the back garden Flora stopped short. "That dratted cat is in our yard again. Maurice will simply have to do something."

Lulu slipped out of the chair, went to the window. "Where is he?" She saw him, and said with a trace of wonder, "He's just a little kitty!"

Flora said in her quick clear voice, "He's a dreadful nuisance. He chases birds, he digs up the flowers and leaves his messes." She flung open a side window, thrust out her head. "*Hist! Hist! Shoo!* You nasty cat! Go away!"

A child's voice sounded faintly from beyond the back fence. "Here Purr, here Purr, here Purr…"

The kitten jerked, frisked sideways, trotted to the back fence, sprang to the top, and over.

Flora slowly closed the window, as if dissatisfied with so easy a victory. She turned back to Lulu. "I suppose you read?"

Lulu reflected a moment. "I read English better than Japanese."

Flora sniffed. "We have a great many books in this house, as you can see." She gestured to the bookcases in various quarters of the room. "Some of them are quite unsuitable for children, so please ask me when you wish to read."

Lulu, considering the dark gold-stamped backs ranged precisely along the cases, thought it unlikely that any of the volumes would interest her. She had not the remotest inkling as to why one of these drab volumes should be 'unsuitable' — unless, of course, the words were too hard…Flora had been speaking: "We all respect each other's belongings; we don't touch and we don't pry. The boys have their bedroom upstairs, which of course you'll have no reason to visit..."

From below came the thud of the front door, the murmur of voices. "I think that's all for the moment," said Flora. "And now I think that you can profitably use the next few minutes unpacking your suitcase."

Lulu nodded, and sliding out of the chair went down the hall to her bedroom, while Flora swept downstairs. Lulu paused in the doorway, uncertain, uneasy. From below came the voice of her Uncle Maurice. "Right here, Albert, for the moment...down. Good..." Then there was sibilant murmuring, pitched too low for her ears.

She went into the bedroom, lifted the suitcase to the bed. After a moment's thought, she set it back to the floor, snapped open the clasps, lifted the lid. Her possessions, packed as neatly as she had been able, seemed very paltry and dingy. At Onomichi they had been at least as good as anyone else's...Oh well, thought Lulu, what does it matter. Even had her clothes been pretty...The remainder of the thought came not as a verbalization, but in an image of her Aunt Flora bending over the suitcase, looking down with critically pursed lips. "I don't *either* wet the bed!" muttered Lulu rebelliously. She went to the bureau, tugged at one of the drawers. It refused to open, and all the others were likewise unyielding.

Lulu went out into the hall, slowly descended the stairs. At the landing she stopped, bewildered by what was occurring in the entry hall.

Her trunk had been opened, her belongings had been removed, placed on the lid or on the floor. Maurice stood watching glumly, beside a white-jacketed Filipino. Flora leaned over the trunk, pushing things aside with fastidious fingers, looking, peering. As Lulu watched, she brought out a large white cardboard box which she carried to a table. She spoke in a sibilant undertone to Maurice, who handed her a pair of scissors. Flora cut the strings, then removed the lid, drew out first a wad of excelsior, then crumpled tissue paper, finally a lavender vase.

Step by step, Lulu descended the stairs, her feet silent in the carpet. Maurice became aware of the silent small shape. He cleared his throat uneasily. Flora twisted about, stared at Lulu with eyes like garnets. "I thought you were told to unpack your suitcase."

"The bureau is locked." She came down into the room, but could think of nothing to say. Without conscious formulation she blurted, "Why are you unpacking my trunk?"

Flora's eyes narrowed; her voice was low, with each word given a menacing articulation. "What did you say?"

Tears of futility and despair filled Lulu's eyes. "You're opening my trunk! You said that we didn't touch each other's things!"

Flora opened her mouth, closed it, and shot a challenging side-glance toward Maurice and the Filipino house-boy, both of whom stood like statues. Turning back to Lulu, Flora said in a decisive voice, "We'll have no impudence, Luellen. There's a very good reason for everything I do and the sooner you learn it the better."

Lulu stood helplessly on the steps, fists clenched up against her chest. Flora continued, in an even voice: "Your father sent me this vase. This is why I opened your trunk — to get my vase. Do you understand?"

Lulu could find no words.

Flora took the vase to the camphorwood cabinet, set it beside the Buddha, then went toward the stairs. "Come, I'll open the bureau drawers. Maurice, bring the trunk on up."

Flora went on into the front bedroom and returned with a large bunch of keys. Brushing past Lulu she unlocked the bureau drawers, and drew them open, allowing a great waft of rose sachet to flood the room. The top drawers contained bundles of letters, notebooks, packages tied in red ribbon, newspaper clippings stapled together, pamphlets and magazines. In the lower drawers, Lulu glimpsed satin and silk, lace and brocade. Flora considered a moment, then closed and re-locked the drawers.

"I'll go through these drawers another time."

"Throw it all out," grumbled Maurice, edging through the door with the front of the trunk. "It's nothing but trash."

"Nothing of the sort...Put the trunk right here, by the wall. We'll unpack later. Maurice, do be careful! You're scraping the metal across the floor!"

Maurice straightened up, red in the face from his exertions. Flora told the house-boy, "Thank you, Albert, that will be all."

The Filipino bowed and withdrew. Lulu went to the trunk, tugged at the hasp. Flora said, "Don't bother now, Luellen, we'll be going directly downtown. We've got to find you some clothes."

"I've got clothes!" said Lulu sullenly. "Dresses and coats and everything."

"Yes, I saw some of them," said Flora. "Perhaps they'll be useful for play-clothes. But you'll need clothes for school, and the occasions when people call. You're living with us now, and we're very particular as to how we look and how we behave."

Maurice looked pointedly at his wrist-watch. "I'm afraid I can't drive you. I have an appointment I can't afford to miss."

"What time is your appointment?" asked Flora evenly.

"Well, at two, or thereabouts."

"There'll be plenty of time." Flora went to the door. "Wash your hands and face, Luellen, and freshen yourself up. We'll be leaving in ten minutes."

Maurice looked after her, blowing out his cheeks peevishly. "Blasted woman," he muttered. "Thinks the whole world should stop dead in its tracks every time she raises a finger."

He turned back to Lulu, and his expression became bland. Stepping forward, he patted her on the head. "I suppose you feel pretty lost in all this…Well don't worry, things aren't as bad as they seem. Not with your Uncle Maurice on hand to chase away the spooks and dragons, eh?" Maurice beamed down at the unresponsive blonde head. He patted her shoulder. "Let's see some sunshine in that pretty little face… What? Tears? Come now, this won't do. Not at all. And I'll give you a little hint, a secret just between us two." Maurice lowered his voice to a jocular murmur. "Don't pay any attention to your Aunt Flora; just let her have her way and don't argue with her, and you'll get along fine."

Lulu nodded listlessly, only half-aware of what Maurice was saying.

Flora appeared in the doorway; Maurice dropped his hand from Lulu's shoulder. Flora looked them coldly up and down and said, "Are you quite ready, Luellen? Do you want to visit the bathroom before we go?"

"No," said Lulu in a muffled voice, looking down at the tips of her shoes.

"Make sure now, because we'll be downtown for several hours."

Flora turned away, descended the stairs. Maurice followed her. Lulu looked about the room, at her black suitcase, at the plundered trunk. She drew a deep shuddering sigh, then went out into the hall and down the steps.

What could her father have been thinking of, to send her here, among these strange people? But now — it was done, and there was no help for it. She sighed once more, in wistful resignation.

CHAPTER IV

MAURICE DROVE FLORA AND LULU downtown: across Van Ness Avenue, out Geary to Union Square. In front of the City of Paris he pulled into a loading zone, reached over Flora and opened the door. Flora sat stonily. "Well?" Maurice demanded testily.

"You haven't parked properly."

"There's no need, since I'm not leaving the car."

"I think that you should come with us."

"Confound it, woman!" exploded Maurice. "I've told you twenty times I'm doing no such thing! Can't you take no for an answer?"

"At the very least," Flora said evenly, "you might take us to lunch."

"At one of your tea-rooms? No, thank you. I'll eat a decent lunch at the club."

"And drink and gamble all afternoon with George Wall and Harper Cox."

"I've seen neither in months!" declared Maurice.

Flora shrugged. "We can go to the St. Francis Grill. Or there's the Blue Fox right around the corner."

Maurice ostentatiously controlled his voice. "I suggest that you get out before a policeman comes past. Now scoot. You and Lulu have a nice lunch."

Flora shrugged once more, glanced at her watch. "It is now eleven-forty. We'll be ready to go home at three o'clock. We'll meet you at three in the St. Francis lobby —"

Maurice's voice cracked with the intensity of his feeling.

"Look along the street! Cabs by the hundreds! Ready, anxious, to convey you anywhere you like — Timbuctoo, if my luck would hold."

"There's no reason to be offensive," said Flora. "Especially in front of the child. I detest taxicabs, and you know it. The drivers are all maniacs or worse."

"What utter rot!" spluttered Maurice. "They're as respectable as I am."

Flora gave her brittle little laugh. "In any case I won't take a cab. I simply refuse. Either you meet us at three or you may take us home this very minute."

"I've a better idea," said Maurice grimly. He opened the door at his own side. "You keep the car, I'll take a cab."

Flora turned around to Lulu. "Your uncle is in one of his bad moods; we'll have a much nicer lunch without him!"

She alighted from the car, signaled Lulu out with a quick twitch of the finger and marched away without a backward glance. Maurice reached in back, opened the door for Lulu, gave her a gallant pat on the shoulder as she alighted. "Have a nice lunch."

Lulu nodded and ran off after Flora. Maurice swerved the Lincoln out into the traffic and drove swiftly north toward the Bohemian Club.

Flora glanced sidelong down her nose as Lulu trotted up. "Your Uncle Maurice is very irritable today... But we won't let that disturb us. Are you hungry?"

"Not very."

Flora pursed her lips in something like approval. "I'm just as pleased your uncle didn't come with us. He'll go to his club and stuff himself with great chunks of meat, but we'll have something dainty and nice at Suliman's."

Suliman's was an upstairs tea-room in Maiden Lane, decorated with carved grilles of honey-colored wood, Indian brasses and Chinese rugs. Flora ordered a vegetable curry, *popadoms*, green tea, for herself; creamed chicken and a glass of milk for Lulu.

Awed by the elegance of the surroundings, Lulu ate with great attention to her table manners, sitting perfectly erect on the edge of her chair, legs dangling several inches above the floor. Flora could find nothing to criticize, and after nibbling for a few moments in silence, suddenly focused her attention on Lulu and in her most charming manner began to inquire about Lulu's life in Japan, to which Lulu responded guardedly.

During dessert — date-nut torte in blueberry sauce — Flora once more fell silent. Covertly Lulu studied this handsome unpredictable woman to whom she must accommodate herself. Eight years of life had provided her only a meager stock of human categories, into none of which Aunt Flora conveniently fit.

After lunch they returned to the City of Paris. With bewildering swiftness, with lavish facility, Lulu was fitted out with more clothes than she had ever imagined owning. There were coats, six of them: dark blue, light blue, a red corduroy swagger jacket, a fuzzy camel-hair, a raincoat of a pale green gabardine, a dark gray tweed with a black fur collar and black fur cap to match. There were dresses: two dozen dresses. Shoes of every description. Skirts, sweaters, pedal-pushers, socks, underwear, blouses: the works. Flora ordered with casual arrogance, the saleswoman murmuring an obsequious obligato, while Lulu stumbled in and out of the dressing room. Flora made not even a pretense of inquiring Lulu's own preferences; the saleswoman, after a few perfunctory pleasantries, entirely ignored her, and her function thereupon became that of a small half-dazed mannequin.

Lulu wore one of the outfits home: a dark green dress with a white scalloped collar, white shoes and dark green socks. The saleswoman brought from the dressing room the navy blue jumper, the white blouse, the little brown oxfords; Flora wrinkled her nose as if they smelled badly, and made a small gesture of dismissal with her fingers. The saleswoman bowed in agreement and the disreputable garments disappeared. Lulu watched them go with a lump in her throat. In Japan these had been her best school clothes.

They left the store and returned to the street, where Flora without visible distress signaled a taxi-cab.

Lulu got in, gingerly leaned back into the cushions and clasped her hands in her lap.

Flora gave crisp directions to the driver and sank back into the seat. She looked at Lulu. "Well — how do you like your lovely new clothes?"

"They're very nice, Aunt Flora. I like them awfully." And after a hesitation, she added, "Thank you very much."

Flora gave her head a little nod, conveying the idea that Lulu's expression of gratitude, while unnecessary, was at the same time rather dilatory. "You're a very lucky little girl, you know."

Lulu blinked. "'Lucky'?"

"Yes," said Flora. "You have a wonderful aunt and uncle to take you into their home and give you advantages you'd never even dream of in Japan."

Lulu nodded uncertainly. Flora continued. "All over the world poor little children who don't have aunts and uncles are starving to death. Of course some are allowed in orphan asylums —"

Lulu knit her brows in patent lack of comprehension.

"An orphan asylum," said Flora, "is a big building where children are kept whose fathers and mothers have died."

"Oh," said Lulu. She looked out of the window. "I guess it's like the camp we were in during the war." She shuddered. "It wasn't very nice."

"Hmmf," sniffed Flora. "It all could have been avoided. We warned your father to leave Japan, but he insisted on staying…Your father was a very obstinate man."

Lulu looked doubtfully at her aunt. She thought she knew what 'obstinate' meant, but something must be wrong; her father had never seemed 'obstinate'.

"Uncle Maurice — is he 'obstinate' too?" Lulu hazarded diffidently.

Flora sounded her crystalline tinkle of a laugh. "Men are very much alike. Yes, quite alike. Vain as peacocks, but really very clumsy, and all obsessed with their carnal appetites…Matters I'm sure you know nothing about."

The allusion, thought Lulu, was probably to her Uncle Maurice's lunch: 'great chunks of meat', as her aunt had put it. "In Japan," said Lulu, thinking to advance the conversation, "people eat *sashimi* — that's raw fish."

"So I understand." Flora glanced out the window. "You'll soon be meeting your cousins Kendall and Oliver. I think you'll like them; they're both fine boys."

Lulu was mildly interested. "How old are they?"

"Kendall is sixteen, Oliver is thirteen."

But when they arrived home Kendall and Oliver were nowhere in evidence. Flora paused in the hall. "You'd better keep on unpacking your trunk," she told Lulu. "We've got to organize ourselves as quickly as possible."

"What shall I do with my clothes?" Lulu asked. "The bureau is full of old papers."

Flora darted her a suspicious glance, then said, "Lay your things neatly on the bed. Then we'll move the trunk out and bring up the oak bureau from the basement."

Lulu climbed the stairs to the second floor, where she could hear a murmur of voices from the third floor. They rose suddenly in pitch. "Give it back, I need it!" "I need it too." "It's mine…Damn it all, you broke it! I'll get yours and break yours!" "You do and I'll break your head."

Lulu went quietly into her room and quietly began to unpack her trunk.

A few minutes later feet thudded down the stairs. There was a sudden brief silence, then Lulu's door was thrust open. Two faces appeared in the doorway, appraising Lulu with merciless candor.

A faint cool quiver ran along the skin of Lulu's back, an odd sensation which she had never known before. She studied the two boys over her shoulder. Clearly they were brothers: both were tall and loose-jointed with narrow shoulders, large hands and feet. Both had dust-colored hair, fresh pink and white complexions, round agate-blue eyes and small heavy-lipped mouths—but here the resemblance ended. Kendall's face was thin and severe; his nose was thin, acerb; his jaw was long, bony, rather oddly angled. Oliver was constructed of softer flesh, of bones less brittle. His face was round, his eyes were almost owlish; his hair was a fleece finer than Kendall's stiff brush.

"Hi," said Kendall tonelessly. "Hi," said Oliver.

"Hi," said Lulu.

The boys came a few steps into the room. Kendall looked into the trunk, then at the bed. "Gee. What a lot of stuff." His voice was condescending, tolerant.

Lulu made no response.

Oliver picked up a book. "This is written in Japanese."

"It's a story book," said Lulu.

"Can you read it?"

"Most of it. Some of the words I don't know."

"Hmmf. Looks like chicken-tracks," said Kendall.

Oliver asked, "Can you speak Japanese?"

"Yes."

"Say something."

"*Watashi no oji Maurice no ichi wa hiro arimasu.*"

"What's that mean?"

"It means, this house — that Uncle Maurice's house is very big."

"Oh."

Flora appeared in the doorway. "Getting acquainted, I see." She looked around the room. "What a confusion! But it can't be helped, I suppose. Boys, do you think you could take this trunk down to the basement?"

"It's a heavy old thing," said Oliver, kicking at the end.

Kendall grabbed one of the handles. "Come along, let's get it downstairs."

"Easy now. Be very careful," Flora warned them. "Especially on the stairs!" She turned and went to the bed. "What's this?" Reaching, she picked up a heavy black loose-leaf ledger.

"It's a photograph album. Daddy gave it to me."

"Well, well." Flora opened it, flicked over the pages.

"There are pictures of you in there," said Lulu, "when you were a little girl, with my mother."

"Well, well." Flora's tone had become cooler. "I'll look at it later." She glanced around the room. "There's nothing much more you can do until we get the bureau in here. Would you like to take a nap?"

Lulu shook her head. "I'm not sleepy."

"Very well. Do just as you wish."

Lulu wandered out into the sitting-room, knelt on the sofa which backed up to the big window overlooking the bay. It was now late afternoon. Sunlight slanted in through the Golden Gate, tinting the white walls of the city, flashing on windows.

Motion caught her eye in the garden below, a small black shadow, jerking, jumping, dodging. Lulu focused her eyes and identified the shadow as a kitten playing with a leaf. Then, looking beyond, where a shaft of sunlight penetrated the rather dingy back yard of the house on the street below, she saw a boy in blue jeans and a blue and green plaid shirt sitting at a picnic table. In front of him lay a notebook in which he wrote, slowly and thoughtfully. A maple tree grew by the fence and a drooping branch obscured the boy's head. As he shifted his position Lulu glimpsed a thin white face, dark eyebrows, dark hair, hollow eye-sockets in which eyes seemed to burn like fire-opals. Lulu watched with mild interest. The boy looked about thirteen years old and evidently was doing homework from school. He appeared frail and unhealthy, and Lulu felt a remote compassion...She thought of her father, who had looked frail and haggard when last she saw him — *and I'll never see him again, never, ever, ever*...Her eyes moistened, she winked back the tears. When he had put her on the boat she had known this in her heart of hearts, and the grief had spent its ardor during the long trip across the Pacific. This would be her new life; already the old times had receded.

Kendall entered the room, came and stood beside her. From certain angles his face looked harsh and aquiline and he seemed much older than sixteen; in other circumstances he appeared no more mature than Oliver. "What're you looking at?" asked Kendall.

"Just outside. Over the bay."

Oliver came into the room eating a banana. Kendall's thin nose wrinkled in an expression identical to one of Flora's. He returned to Lulu. "See that island out there? That's Alcatraz."

"Oh? What are all those big houses?"

Kendall laughed. " 'Big houses' is right. That's the federal pen. Al Capone is there right now. Maybe he's looking right out at us."

Lulu had no idea who Al Capone might be, but thought it best to conceal her ignorance.

Oliver moved forward and the rich odor of masticated banana enveloped Lulu. "You've got blonde hair," announced Oliver. He gave one of her pigtails a tug. "How come?"

Lulu twisted around, surveyed the owl-eyed Oliver with dignity. "How come what?"

"How come you're blonde? I thought Japanese people had black hair."

"I'm not Japanese."

"Sure you are. You were born in Japan."

This was Kendall speaking, in a light dry voice. Lulu surveyed him carefully. "Weren't you born in China?"

Kendall shifted his glance to the window. "What if I was? I'm not a Chinaman."

"I didn't say you were," said Lulu.

Kendall's attention had been diverted. "Look. There's the old pro. Old Professor Chickweed."

"What's he doing?" Oliver kneeled on the couch, pressed his nose to the glass. "Writing in his book."

"What is he writing?" asked Lulu.

Neither Kendall nor Oliver chose to answer; Kendall went to the side window on three long gliding steps. He eased back the latch, swung the window out a stealthy three inches. Putting his mouth to the crack, he called out, "Hey, Chickweed! Chickweed the freak!" Stepping swiftly back, he hooked the window shut.

Lulu watched open-mouthed. Then she looked down over the garden. The boy in the sunlight had turned, and was staring up at the windows of the Brewer house.

Lulu sat back on the couch, lowered her head, studied her hands. Flora came down the hall. "Who in the world is shouting so?"

"It was me," stated Kendall, with noble simplicity.

"It was 'I', please. And I don't care to have you shouting down at that boy."

"His cat's in our yard again," offered Oliver.

Flora clicked her tongue and went to the window. She shook her head in annoyance. "The boy must know what a nuisance he's causing… Now it's climbing the cabbage palm."

"I'll fix it," said Kendall grimly. "I'll get my .22 and shoot it where it'll do the most good."

"You'll do no such thing," declared Flora. "You're not to shoot that gun. Unless your father is present."

Kendall's face drooped dourly. "I'm not exactly a child, you know."

Lulu looked at him wonderingly. *I'm not exactly a child.* The sentence rang in her mind. *I'm not a child. Not exactly.* Kendall became aware of her attention and scowled down at her.

Oliver said in a helpful voice, "There's my slingshot. We could use my slingshot…"

The boy in the yard below had become aware of the regard focused on him. He looked around him, craning his neck, and through the glass Lulu saw him calling. The kitten sprang up the fence, hopped down upon the dingy concrete paving. The boy scratched its head; the kitten bobbed and danced.

"Is he sick?" asked Lulu.

"We don't really know," said Flora carelessly.

Oliver said knowledgeably, "He got run over, and then he got bone cancer and now he's going to die, because it's incurable."

"Nonsense," said Flora in disgust. "Nothing of the sort. He's merely a sickly eccentric child."

"His father works in a garage," said Kendall. "He might have been cured if his father didn't gamble. Now they don't have any money and Chickweed's jazz is a thing of the past."

"Kendall!" snapped Flora. "Must you talk like that?"

He's not exactly a child, thought Lulu.

"There goes Chickweed," said Oliver, "taking his cat and his book inside."

"Something will have to be done about that cat," said Flora rather vaguely. From below came the thud of the front door closing. She turned swiftly and marched downstairs.

"Father's home," said Kendall. "Probably with a load on."

Oliver said wisely, "Whenever Father comes home from the club — watch out!"

Lulu looked from one to the other in astonishment. Such cynicism! Such worldliness! Such disrespect! ... She assured herself that she had misunderstood. Meanwhile something else was troubling her.

"That boy down there —"

"Professor Chickweed?"

"Is that his name?"

"Certainly that's his name. Chickweed."

Lulu licked her lips. "Is he really going to die?"

"We're all going to die," Oliver stated grandly. "Some day."

"I mean, is he going to die — right away?"

"Naw," said Kendall brassily. "Do you think we'd tease him and call him names if he was really going to die?"

Lulu remained dissatisfied, for a reason she could not define. After a moment of chewing her lip she asked, "How do you know he's not going to die? I mean, if you heard that he was sick —"

"Gad! What a persistent little devil!" cried Kendall.

Lulu, looking into his suddenly passionate high-nosed face, thought, *he is not exactly a child*... But he was hardly larger than Oliver — who still carried wads and lumps of baby fat with him.

Footsteps sounded on the stairs.

"Here he comes," said Kendall gloomily. "Should I hit him up now, while he's still got a heat on? He might clout me. Should I wait till he's got a hangover and can't think of anything else?"

"He might still clout you."

"Yeah."

Maurice came in from the hall, lurching the least bit, but contriving a brave swagger. Behind came Flora, frozen-faced with disgust and disapproval.

Kendall put the issue to an immediate test. "Say, Dad."

Maurice twisted about. Only the opacity of his eyes, the high pink shine of his cheeks and forehead, indicated that Maurice had been over-indulging. Until he spoke, and then his voice was thick. "Well then, Kendall, my boy?"

Kendall took courage at the jovial tone. "I wonder if I could have the car tonight?"

Kendall was much too young to be driving, thought Lulu. In Japan only very important personages drove cars.

Flora seemed to think along the same lines because she drew her lips into a thin pale line and shook her head. Maurice, observing, reared back his head, raised his bushy eyebrows, turned his back on Flora. "Ha ha! So. A bit of sparking, eh boy? Or a night at the opera? Which?"

"Well, it's not the opera."

"Ha ha! And who's the lucky girl?"

Kendall hesitated. "I don't think you know her. Just a girl at school."

Oliver said with subtle malice, "Father knows her. Nancy Tully. She's editor of *Polychrome*."

"Oho!" Maurice's eyebrows rose and wagged comically. "That one! Hotsy totsy!"

"She's much too old for Kendall," said Flora rather sharply. "Seventeen, easily. I really don't approve."

Kendall turned a burning glance of hatred at Oliver, then carefully composed his face. "She's only just seventeen, and really she's a very nice girl. After all, she's editor of the literary magazine."

"Yes," said Flora with a faint sniff. "I've seen the magazine. Things have certainly changed since I was young."

Lulu, understanding nothing of what was going on, looked back and forth between Flora and Kendall.

Kendall said in a disgusted voice, "Good heavens, Mother, we're only going to a party. A quiet civilized party."

"And there'll be drinking." Flora turned a spiteful glance toward Maurice. "And the very cheapest sort of behavior." But here she overplayed her hand; Maurice snorted, threw his hands over his head. "Go, my son," he said loftily. "When I was your age — ha ha!"

Flora marched from the room. Maurice shook his head in wonder. "An extraordinary woman. Can't understand her, never could…"

Kendall struck while the iron was hot. "May I have the keys now, Father?"

Maurice reluctantly fished a key ring from his pocket. "It's against my better judgment." He weighed the keys in his hand. "Mind you, drive carefully."

"Yes, sir."

"When are you leaving?"

"Right after dinner."

"And when will you be home?"

Kendall pursed his lips. "That's hard to say. Not too late, of course," he said hastily as the mulish pout came to Maurice's mouth.

"No drinking and driving. Get me?"

Kendall nodded eagerly, then sensing an ambiguity, shook his head. "I'll be careful."

Dinner was stiff and quiet, except for Oliver's inconsequential chatter.

Maurice, his exaltation dissolved, hulked morosely at the head of the table; Flora picked at a salad. Kendall sat with ostentatious rectitude, frowning as Oliver lounged and squirmed beside him. Lulu was ignored, but she was too tired to notice.

Kendall had already dressed for his date in a neat blue suit, a striped shirt, a dull red tie. At his wrist glittered a gold chainlink watch-band which he inspected pridefully from time to time. Lulu thought he looked very grown-up and almost handsome, in a thin-faced satanic sort of way. Kendall definitely felt very pleased with himself. Flora, watching him from the corner of her eye, at last gave a faint ladylike snort. "I can't conceive why you bought that watch-band. It's really rather flashy."

Kendall looked up, startled. " 'Flashy'? No such thing! It's gold! I paid eight dollars for it, with my own money!"

Oliver chuckled unctuously. "Kendall must be sick; he spent his own money."

"Shut up," muttered Kendall.

"He's so tight he squeaks," Oliver told Lulu.

Kendall glared. He opened his mouth in rebuttal, but Flora's voice came at him from the other side. "You should have bought a nice leather strap like your father's. They're in much better taste."

Kendall almost visibly retreated into himself, like a turtle withdrawing into its shell. He said in surly defiance, "I like it; that's why I bought it."

Flora gave her shoulders a little shrug and looked off in another direction.

Dessert was served: apple cobbler in cinnamon sauce, which Oliver sprinkled liberally with sugar before consuming. "No wonder he's such a fat slob," sneered Kendall, looking down his nose, but Oliver merely grinned and scraped up the last of the syrup.

Lulu's eyes were drooping; the day had been very eventful. Maurice noticed and chuckled ripely.

"Yes," said Flora crisply. "Just a trifle grubby too." She rose to her feet. "Come, Luellen, let's go run a bath for you, and then you can go to bed."

Lulu dutifully followed Flora up the stairs to the second floor, where Flora said, "You run in and find your cleanest pajamas, and bring them up to the boys' bathroom."

"They're all clean," muttered Lulu peevishly.

Flora snapped her fingers. "Just do as you're told and no impudence." She went on up to the third floor.

Lulu defiantly took the first pair of pajamas she found and marched on upstairs to the bathroom. Flora had started the water and was laying out a towel.

"Scrub very well," said Flora. "All over. And you had better wash your hair too." She departed, closing the door behind her.

Lulu undressed, climbed into the tub. The warm water relaxed her, she almost fell asleep. But this would never do; if she were too long Flora would be up to ask what was keeping her. She loosened her braids, ducked herself, rubbed soap into her hair...Horror of horrors! the door opened to reveal Oliver's grinning face. Lulu squeaked in dismay. She had neglected to twist the lock, and Oliver thereby wrought more mischief than he had planned. He said coarsely, "Why don't you lock the door, embarrassing me like this?"

"Go away," cried Lulu, hugging herself.

"You're kinda skinny, aren't you?" said Oliver and nonchalantly departed, leaving the door open. Lulu jumped up, and in an agony of haste lest Oliver should reappear, slammed and locked the door; then continued her bath tingling with humiliation. "I hate it here!" she whispered. "I hate it, hate it, hate it!"

Soaped, scrubbed, rinsed and dried, wearing her pink pajamas and old terry-cloth bathrobe, she opened the door cautiously, half-expecting to find Oliver waiting for her. But the hall was vacant. Lulu ran down the steps to her own room. She turned out the lights and flung herself into the sachet-scented bed.

A moment later the lights were snapped back on. Flora stood in the doorway. "Did you scrub yourself really well?"

"Yes, Aunt Flora."

"And did you polish out the tub?"

"Yes."

"Very well. Good night."

"Good night."

The light snapped out, the door closed.

Lulu relaxed into the strange bed. "I wish I were in Japan," she whispered. "I wish Daddy were still here..." A lump rose in her throat, tears ran down her cheeks, and presently she fell asleep.

CHAPTER V

SHORTLY BEFORE TWO in the morning Kendall side-swiped a parked car on Sloat Boulevard. The din of squealing tires and collapsing metal seemed deafening. Kendall halted one petrified instant, then looking backward and forward along the street shifted into low and raced the Lincoln madly away.

The girl beside him giggled hysterically. "Oh Lord, this is everything! And I can't find my pants … Kendall, find my pants; you had them last."

"Devil take your pants," said Kendall between clenched teeth.

"That's a very self-centered attitude," said the girl. "If they were your pants you'd be looking around on your hands and knees."

"Not on your life," said Kendall. "Instead of driving I'd be flying. I want to get away from here fast. Preferably with my pants on. I'm a dead duck now if the cops catch me."

"Not a dead duck," said the girl drowsily. "A drunk duck."

"I'm also a gone goose," said Kendall bleakly, "when they see that front end." The mental picture was appallingly vivid; his voice dwindled.

He delivered the girl to her apartment and drove home, crouched and shrunken over the wheel. What a cataclysm! Should he swagger in and break the news tonight? Or wait till the morning? All hell was sure to break loose. And Kendall gnawed his lips.

The house showed only a dim yellow glow from the entry-hall. Kendall slipped inside, stole like a shadow up the stairs.

As Kendall undressed in the dark, Oliver spoke in a thick drowsy voice, "Well, big-shot, how did you make out?"

"Shut up," said Kendall huskily.

Oliver grunted without resentment and dropped back off to sleep.

The night passed; morning came. In a would-be casual voice Kendall broke the news. The reaction substantiated all his misgivings: doubly, triply so when Flora discovered the misplaced pants under the front seat and noticed a streak of alcoholic vomit down the side of the car.

Lulu was ignored and wandered curiously around the periphery of the tumult. Maurice displayed the most vehemence, and Lulu marveled at his choler. With clinical detachment she studied the crimson vibration of his jowls, the furious gestures, the agitated stalking back and forth. Presently she told herself wisely, "He's mad because he thinks Kendall fooled him." Her Aunt Flora's conduct was more complex. The waspish reproaches, the searching questions were not unexpected, but Lulu seemed to glimpse an underlying satisfaction, so secret and indefinable that Lulu could not be sure it really existed. It was a puzzling situation. Kendall evidently had conducted himself in a depraved manner: there had been drinking, and naughtiness of a more mysterious and fascinating nature, as exemplified by the disembodied pants. Why, Lulu asked herself, should Aunt Flora seem secretly pleased?

If Uncle Maurice had been at fault, then all could be explained: Aunt Flora would have been jealous and happy that the evening had ended in grief. But Kendall…Was it possible that Aunt Flora was jealous with Kendall too, and disliked having him show attention to other ladies? Perhaps this was why Aunt Flora seemed to dislike Lulu herself. Lulu could conceive not even the remotest cause for jealousy in connection with herself. Although Uncle Maurice seemed to like her, and had even said she was pretty. It was puzzling.

Lulu abandoned the analysis. Somewhere close at hand lay the motive for Aunt Flora's barely-glimpsed gloating. It was far past Lulu's conscious understanding, although the dim regions of her instinctive mind tingled and tickled with ageless wisdom.

The first furious uproar finally subsided and gave place to a silence bitter as bile. Lulu lost interest in the affair and wandered down into the back garden.

And there was the black kitten, as Lulu had hoped. He sat under a hydrangea, apparently at his ease, but when Lulu approached he bounded away, tail twisted off to the side. Lulu looked across the fence but the back-yard was vacant. She found a twig, scratched at the ground, and presently teased the kitten into chasing the tip. Back, forth, pausing, darting, ran the kitten. Lulu pivoted, swinging the tip of the twig in a circle, and the kitten scurried around the circumference, until Lulu became dizzy. She reeled against the maple tree, while the kitten sprawled out on the lawn.

In an upstairs window of the house across the fence a white face glimmered briefly. Lulu craned her neck but Professor Chickweed had drawn back out of sight.

Lulu approached the kitten on hands and knees, stroked the soft black back. The kitten paraded back and forth, carrying its tail like a battle standard... From the corner of her eye, Lulu glimpsed motion, a flicker of dark blue and green.

Professor Chickweed had come from the house. He crossed the yard and tentatively approached the fence, limping as he walked.

"Hello," said Lulu primly.

"Hi." He chirruped to the kitten. "Come here, you fool cat."

The kitten paid him no heed. Lulu lifted him and carried him to the fence. Professor Chickweed seemed even thinner and paler at close range. "What's his name?"

"Purr." He took the cat. "Stupid animal. You're not supposed to go in that yard, do you hear?"

"Cats don't mind very well," said Lulu. "I had a big tabby cat, but I couldn't bring it here. It had quarantines."

Professor Chickweed glanced at her sidewise. "It had what?"

"Quarantines. It's some kind of — something. I couldn't bring it here on account of it."

"I never heard of it."

"I never did before either. Kip seemed very healthy too."

Professor Chickweed gave Lulu a swift and careful scrutiny. "Who are you?"

"I'm Lulu Enright. I've come here to live."

"Are you related to —" Professor Chickweed nodded toward the house "— them?"

"Kendall and Oliver? They're my cousins. My father is dead, so I had to come here. But I'd rather be back in Japan."

Professor Chickweed once more looked up toward the back of the Brewer house. "I don't wonder."

Lulu asked innocently, "Is your real name Chickweed?"

The boy's face pinched and became even paler. "What difference does it make?"

Lulu, looking into the glowing black eyes, sensed possibilities she had never before even suspected. She became a little frightened. "It doesn't make any difference," she stammered hurriedly. "Not to me... Kendall said it was your name."

The boy relaxed a trifle. "You must be pretty dumb."

Lulu took no offense. But the boy had neither affirmed nor denied his name. Was he ashamed of it? Best to pursue the matter no further. Except in one regard. Pitching her voice in a tone of friendly curiosity she asked, "But why do they call you Professor?"

The boy chuckled bitterly. "That's the least thing they call me."

"I'll call you Chick. That's short for Chickweed."

The boy stared coldly a moment, then grunted. "I don't care what you call me. I don't care about anything or anybody." He limped back away from the fence, seated himself at the picnic table, rested his head broodingly on his hand.

Lulu, hanging on the fence, watched him in fascination. "Chick!"

"Don't call me Chick."

Lulu blinked in perplexity. "What should I call you?"

"I don't care."

"Then," said Lulu, "I'll call you Chick."

"All right, then, call me Chick."

"What are you writing in that book?"

"Ask your stupid cousins."

Lulu looked over her shoulder. "They wouldn't tell me." She added, "Kendall wrecked the car last night. He took some pants away from a girl, and everybody's mad at him. He's in disgrace and he can't use the car ever again... You didn't answer me."

"Didn't answer what?"

Lulu said patiently, "I asked what you're writing."

Chick fixed her with his dark brooding gaze. "Why do you want to know? So you can tell your cousins?"

"No. I really don't like them very much."

"I'm writing a Book of Dreams."

Lulu became instantly charmed. She pressed closer against the fence. "Dreams that you've dreamed?"

"No. Dreams that I make up...I suppose you'll tell them."

"Oh no!"

"Not that I care. I don't care what they do. Or what you do."

"I won't tell."

Chick shrugged.

"You're sick, aren't you?" asked Lulu.

"I guess so," said Chick gloomily.

"What kind of sickness is it?"

"Nobody knows." He gave a quick bark of laughter.

"But you'll be getting better," said Lulu comfortingly. "It's summer. People always get better when it's summer."

"I hope so...Do you want to know something?"

"What?"

"Everybody says I'm going to die."

Lulu's mouth became a shocked O. "Are you? Really?"

"I don't know. Sometimes I think so."

"But aren't you scared?"

"I don't really believe it. The doctor says I'm getting better."

"Oh, I hope so! I really do!"

Chick looked past her, up to the top of the yard. "Here they come. Purr? Where's Purr? Come here, Purr."

Kendall trudged slowly down the path, followed by Oliver. They saw Lulu and slowed their pace. Kendall made a hoarse cawing sound. "Hey, what's this? Lulu's got herself a boy friend."

"I guess it's going to be Mr. and Mrs. Chickweed," said Oliver.

"She's young," said Kendall, "but she's a fast worker."

Lulu wondered how she could ever have thought Kendall seemed grown-up and rather handsome. Now he looked just a rather saturnine youth, ungainly and unpleasant. She said clearly, "You two boys aren't very nice."

"Piffle," said Oliver. He flipped a pebble into the air. "Who wants to be nice?...What's the matter Chickweed? Where are you going?"

Chick had hoisted himself to his feet. "I'm going inside."

"Can't take it, eh?"

"Come here, Purr." Chick went around the table. "Let's go inside." The kitten perversely scampered away and jumped over the fence.

"Look," cried Oliver in mock outrage. "There's that cat again."

"Chase it out of here," Kendall ordered. "Kick it right over the fence."

"No," cried Lulu, shocked. She ran forward, picked up the kitten. Oliver intercepted her before she could reach the fence. "Let's have that cat," said Oliver. He seized it. Lulu tried to twist away, the kitten cried out. Chick pattered up to the fence. "Don't hurt him! Please don't hurt him."

"Let go," said Oliver. "Let go, Lulu! Or there'll be two half-cats!"

Lulu had to relinquish the frightened kitten, which in trying to escape clawed Oliver's hand. "Why, you mean little devil!" exclaimed Oliver.

Chick called out, "Give him to me!"

Oliver looked to Kendall, who had stretched disinterestedly out on the lawn. "What'll I do to it, Ken? Strangle it?"

"Turn it inside out."

Lulu ran forward. "Don't you dare!"

"Give me my cat!" raved Chick. "I'll have you arrested, I'll put you in jail!"

"Ha ha! The cat's on our property, we can have *you* arrested, because we told you to keep him off. So…Ouch! Dirty little beast!"

The kitten scratched and bit and fought its way out of Oliver's grasp. Oliver ran forward, but Lulu stood in his way, and Purr escaped over the fence. Chick scooped him up and with a single backward glance limped across the yard and inside his house.

Oliver nursed his scratches. "I'll kill that cat. I'll shoot him."

"Not with my gun," said Kendall. "I'm in enough trouble now."

"I'll use my slingshot. Next time I see that cat."

Lulu said indignantly, "Why can't you be nice to Chick? He isn't hurting you."

"He's weird."

"He's sick!"

"Rats," said Kendall disgustedly. "He's no sicker than I am. It's a big act. Last week I saw him dancing with that cat."

"He just wants attention," was Oliver's opinion.

Kendall sat up. He focused his eyes. "Look! He left that book he's always scribbling in. Let's get it and see what he's written."

Oliver went to the fence, started to climb it. Lulu stood stock-still, her heart frozen, her mind crawling with an emotion she had never felt before. She acted without conscious thought. Taking a deep breath, she stepped forward, quiet, almost demure. She picked up a stake where it lay beside the path, swung it as hard as she could against Oliver's plump buttocks. Kendall guffawed in pure pleasure, Oliver squealed and lunged murderously for Lulu. She raised the stake, brought it down with both hands. It glanced off Oliver's temple; there was a sudden torrent of blood.

Oliver wailed in terror and rage, and lurched blindly forward. Kendall ducked nimbly in behind Lulu, grabbed for the stake. Lulu pulled at his arm, caught her fingers under the new gold watch-band. It stretched and parted; the watch lay on the lawn, a poor spangle, a pride destroyed.

The three stood panting, Oliver pressing his hands to his head. "My God," husked Kendall in awe. "You're *vicious*!" He looked down at his watch, felt his left wrist. "That cost eight dollars!" he said. "My own money."

Oliver ran on tottery feet for the house. Kendall picked up his watch and with a grim glance for Lulu, followed.

From the house over the fence came Chick. He went to the table, picked up his book, returned inside. Lulu watched him dumbly. Then with leaden feet she walked up the path toward the house.

She climbed the back steps, went through the pantry into the kitchen. Here she paused a long moment, then diffidently pushed open the swinging door and sidled into the dining room where she paused again.

In the entry hall were Oliver, Kendall, her Aunt Flora and Uncle Maurice. Oliver stood on a sheet of newspaper someone had spread to protect the floor, while Maurice swabbed his wound with a cotton pad and pressed to control the bleeding. At the telephone Flora spoke decisively to someone who appeared to be angry. Kendall stood to the side, and was the first to notice Lulu. "Here she is," he said simply.

Flora hung up the phone, and looked for a few long seconds at Lulu. Then, with a deliberation which was more menacing than a scream of rage, she turned away and spoke in a calm cold voice to Maurice. "Doctor Knapp is on his way. He says to stay where we are, not to move Oliver." She glanced once more toward Lulu, who now came slowly forward.

Maurice shook his head at her in disappointment and disapproval. Flora said in a voice like an icicle, "Well, young lady, what do you have to say for yourself?"

Lulu could think of nothing to say. She hung her head. In retrospect her offense had grown to enormous proportions. Never before in her life had she done anything so violent, but this would have no meaning for her Aunt Flora. Worse, she could find no words to explain her action; in fact, she hardly knew herself.

"Well?" asked Flora. "Please answer me, Luellen."

Maurice said uncomfortably, "Oh come now, Flora, don't be too hasty. The young scoundrel probably got no more than he deserved."

"I was only climbing the fence," Oliver cried out passionately, "and she bangs me with a big stick!"

"Is this true, Luellen?"

Lulu nodded miserably. "I didn't mean to hurt him…"

Kendall spoke in his grown-up voice, "I tried to stop her. I got my hands on the stick, but she wouldn't let go. She tore off my watch, broke my new band."

Flora glanced up at Maurice with an odd sweet-sour smile. "Well?"

"I still say there's two sides to every story, and we haven't heard hers."

"You're certainly very gallant," said Flora. "Very gallant, very noble."

"Nothing of the sort," said Maurice stiffly. "I resent your attitude."

"My attitude is perfectly clear. This young person made an entirely unprovoked attack upon Oliver. He was climbing the fence. It had nothing to do with her. It was a vicious thing to do."

Maurice turned to Lulu. "What about it? Were these two rascals tormenting you?"

"We were not!" chorused Kendall and Oliver.

Maurice turned on them. "Then why did she pick up the stick?"

"I don't know," said Oliver smugly.

Lulu found her tongue. "He was going after Chick's book. He…He was going to tear it up." Lulu wanted to say that she could not bear to have Kendall and Oliver snickering over Chick's Book of Dreams, but she knew that Maurice would fail to understand and that Flora would willfully misunderstand.

The doorbell rang; Flora admitted a short fat man in a dark suit. He set down his little black satchel, moved Oliver to the light. "A few stitches and we'll be as good as new…"

Flora turned to Lulu. "Go to your room. You'll have no lunch and only bread and milk for dinner."

As Lulu walked leadenly to the steps she heard Kendall complain, "What about my watch-band?"

"That's something you'll have to arrange with Luellen."

Kendall followed Lulu up the stairs. Lulu went to her room, sat down on the bed, hands clenched between her knees. Kendall looked in the doorway. "You'll have to pay for that watchband," he said. "Eight dollars. It was brand new."

Lulu shook her head. "It was your own fault."

"You broke it, and you're going to pay."

Lulu said nothing.

"You've got money," said Kendall. "It's not fair that you break my things. I want eight dollars."

"All right, that's enough," said a gruff voice. Maurice loomed over Kendall. "As soon as you finish paying for the damage to the car, Lulu can pay you for your watch-band. It's costing you about a hundred dollars."

Kendall gaped in dismay. "A hundred dollars."

"That's right. The insurance doesn't cover because you were driving. So — I'll take a hundred dollars from your allowance. Or you can give it to me in cash. I know you've got it, you've been hoarding for years."

Kendall thoughtfully left the room. Maurice came in, looked behind him down the hall, half-closed the door, sat down on the bed. Lulu was now lying face down, limp and passive.

"Tsk, tsk," clicked Maurice. "Shoes on the bed. Flora would have something more to say." He untied the laces, pulled the shoes from Lulu's feet. Lulu lay quiet, although her skin tingled and prickled.

"Now," said Maurice, "What's all this about? I suppose those two young devils were ragging you?"

To a certain degree this was true, reflected Lulu. She jerked her head in affirmation.

"Well," said Maurice, "boys will be boys, as the saying goes. These particular two…Well, I suppose they're about like any other two. But the main thing is that we're all living in this house and we've all got to get along…" Maurice continued in this vein for several minutes. "And above all, don't forget —" here he gave her bottom a playful pat "— that whenever you want something, you come tell me. Get it? When there's problems just let me know, and by Jingo, we'll get 'em fixed." He gave her another little spank, and left his hand familiarly in place. It seemed oppressively heavy. Lulu lay quiet. "So everything's going to be all right," said Maurice. He moved his hand. "There'll be little quarrels and hurt feelings now and then, but I know we can all bear up. And as far as you and I are concerned, it's the old buddy system. Right?"

"All right," said Lulu.

"Fine! Now give your old buddy a kiss. We'll get along even if nobody else does. Come on now, a nice smooch."

Lulu raised up, pecked at his cheek.

"Here now," Maurice protested. "That's not much of a kiss…"

He lifted his head, squinted thoughtfully, rose to his feet. "It's been a bad morning for everybody," said Maurice. "But we'll try to forget it — start over from scratch."

The door swung open. Flora said, "The doctor took five stitches." She glanced quizzically at Lulu. "He wanted to know if Oliver had been in an automobile accident. I was ashamed, naturally, to tell him the truth."

"Now, now," said Maurice gruffly. "That's enough. I've talked to Lulu; we've agreed that she's sorry for what happened. I think we can let it go at that."

"Nevertheless," said Flora stiffly, "she must keep to her room the rest of the day."

Maurice blew out his cheeks. "I hardly feel that —"

Flora interrupted in a silky voice: "Surely there's no need to be quite so solicitous, Maurice?"

Maurice marched from the room. Flora went to the window, touched the curtains, drew the shade. She turned back to Lulu. "Five stitches in Oliver's forehead…You must learn to control your temper. Or someday you'll find yourself in serious trouble."

She departed, closing the door gently after her.

Lulu listened frozen-faced to the retreating footsteps. She thought of her father and some of her bitterness extended to him: how could he have let her come to such a house?

She sat up, swung her legs over the side of the bed, looked around the room. She had never really explored it before. White plaster ceiling, walls papered with a design of red roses on a blue-gray field. Dull Turkey-red carpet. Along one wall the bureau and the contents of her trunk, still piled on the floor. Under the window a long low chest. Along the other wall, first a closet, then her bed. On the walls hung oriental lithographs in black, white, gray and red, depicting incidents from the life of Buddha. And everywhere the cloying odor of rose sachet…The door-knob turned slowly. Lulu watched it in fascination. The lock clicked; the door swung slowly open. Kendall's saturnine face appeared in the gap. The two stared eye to eye, both faces expressionless as insects.

Kendall said huskily, "You think I'm kidding about that eight dollars. I'm not. You owe it to me and I'm going to collect. If I have to take it out of your hide."

Flora could not have been far away. Lulu heard her voice, sharp and clear. "Kendall, what are you doing?"

"I'm talking to Lulu," Kendall grumbled.

"Close the door."

In the hall Kendall spoke further, but his voice was muffled and Lulu caught only snatches: "— eight dollars, not counting tax…chased us away. He acts like we're to blame for everything…"

Flora's voice penetrated more distinctly. "Your father is sometimes headstrong, sometimes even a little foolish. But you should be worrying more about your own conduct. I haven't forgotten, by no means; I never shall. Just plain nastiness, the way cur dogs act. And not to mention the way you damaged the car."

There was no reply from Kendall.

Lulu rose to her feet, went to the window. It overlooked roofs and a small scrap of gray-blue bay. The sun shone brilliantly. Clouds sailed high on the wind. Lulu suddenly felt caged, almost desperate... But this would avail nothing.

She quietly opened the closet. Old clothes, old hat-boxes. Nothing which looked interesting. She went back to her bed, sat down. It was lunch-time. Lulu would have liked a nice sandwich and a glass of milk. Better yet, an ice-cream soda... She wondered what Chick was having for lunch. She felt sorry for Chick. He was being brave, not complaining of how frightened he was that he was going to die...

She went to where her belongings had been piled on the floor, picked up some of the books she had brought with her, and made shift to interest herself.

Time passed. The house seemed very quiet. A sound at the door. Again it opened quietly, this time to reveal Oliver, with a fine bandage on his forehead. He touched it. "You see that? Five stitches." He spoke with a trace of pride. "Look."

"I see it," said Lulu.

"You better see it. Because you got off pretty easy. Too easy. And we're going to get revenge."

"I'll hit you again. Harder. With a bigger stick."

Oliver's eyes bulged. "You know what you are? You're —"

Flora's voice once more broke into the conversation. "Oliver! What are you doing?"

Oliver's voice was mild. "Nothing. I was talking to her. And she said she was going to hit me again."

"Nonsense. Now go away and stop bothering Luellen."

"She's reading."

Flora appeared in the doorway. "No reading, Luellen, that's part of your punishment."

"It's the Bible."

"Oh... Hmmf. Well, I'll make an exception. You may read the Bible."

"I wasn't reading it. I was looking at my pressed flowers."

"Heavens," snorted Flora. "What a thing to do! Didn't your father ever teach you a decent respect for the Bible?"

"No."

"It's one of the great revelations," said Flora. "That's how all our knowledge comes to us. From the Great Central Lotus. It's part of

Christianity, it's part of the Sutras, it's part of everything wise and holy and wonderful. Do you understand what I'm talking about?"

Lulu, who had never learned to dissemble, shook her head.

"The main thing to remember," said Flora, "is that nothing fleshly helps the Soul toward Nirvana. Rich food, drink, carnality — do you know what I mean by carnality?"

Lulu frowned. Whatever her aunt meant by 'carnality' certainly wasn't very nice. She decided she really didn't know, and shook her head.

"Well, it doesn't matter. But the main thing is, if you live by the Four Principles of Good then you draw good vibrations after you."

"Aunt Flora," said Lulu absently. "May I have my vase up here in my room?"

"Vase?" A pinched look came over Flora's handsome features. "What vase?"

"The purple vase you took out of my trunk. I'd like it up here in my room."

"No," said Flora. "Your father and I have an arrangement concerning that vase. It will remain where it is. And," she said as Lulu started to speak, "we won't discuss the matter again."

Lulu bent her head over the flowers. Flora left the room. Lulu sighed dismally. By chance her eyes focused on the print. Out of idle curiosity she read a few verses, but the language was strange, and conveyed nothing of interest. Still, it was supposed to be a very important book, all about God... Lulu returned to her flowers. Presently her eyes felt heavy and she took a nap.

She awoke to mingled excitement, panic and strangeness. Where was she, what was this room smelling so sweet of antique scent? She remembered. Depression flooded back. The sky — as much as could be glimpsed through the window — was dim, suffused with twilight murk. It must be close to dinner time, thought Lulu. Her stomach gurgled. She yawned. A moment later she heard the dinner chimes sounding below in the dining room. She thought, while they're all at dinner I could go down the front stairs, out the door, into the dark — and they'd never find me... But where would I go?

A discreet tap at the door. It swung open; a young Filipino in a white coat came in. This was Giorgio, the latest in an interminable succession of servants. He carried a tray which he put on the bed, grinning at Lulu. "Little girl been bad, eh? Gets dinner in jail."

On the tray was two slices of buttered bread, a glass of milk, a sliced tomato. Giorgio left, Lulu angrily surveyed the tray. Swallowing her pride, she ate. Then going to the door, she opened it a crack, listened. From downstairs the rumble of voices. She stepped out into the hall. From below rose the odor of rich roast beef. Lulu crossed to the bathroom. On the way back she loitered in the hall, feeling daring and defiant and adventurous. Then, hearing the scrape of a chair, she ran back into her room.

With nothing better to do, she undressed, got into her pajamas and climbed into bed.

She lay thinking. In this house I'm really all alone, she told herself. Uncle Maurice acts friendly, but in an odd kind of way. All this kissing stuff…I'd just as soon he weren't so buddy-buddy. Odd. Maybe he's lonesome…Her eyelids drooped. Someday I'll be grown-up, she said drowsily. I'll tell them all to go to…You know where. I'll take my vase and my trunk and just my own clothes and I'll go back to Japan and be a missionary.

She went to sleep.

CHAPTER VI

THE NEXT DAY WAS SUNDAY. Lulu arose with the firm resolve to be polite and formal and pleasant to everyone. She was even sorry she had hit Oliver.

She dressed in one of her new outfits, brushed her hair till it crackled and tied it into a pony-tail. She wanted to brush her teeth very badly — but that meant going upstairs to the boys' bathroom and — well...Taking a grip on her self-possession, she marched upstairs. The boys were still in bed, though awake.

Lulu brushed her teeth, washed her face, and returned downstairs, her dignity intact. From the dining room came the sound of soft chimes. Lulu was glad she was dressed.

Flora was already at the table. "Good morning, Lulu."

"Good morning, Aunt Flora."

Flora gave Lulu a careful scrutiny. "Did you brush your teeth?"

"Yes."

"Hmmf. You look very nice this morning in your new dress."

Lulu took a seat in one of the big carved walnut chairs, and sipped from a glass of orange juice. Flora continued to read the newspaper. Lulu lacked the courage to ask for the funnypapers.

Maurice came heavily downstairs, settled into his chair at the head of the table. "Where are the boys?"

"I'm sure they'll be right down."

"Damned sluggards, both of them."

The house-boy brought in bacon and eggs and toast. Maurice served generously.

"Very little for me," said Flora. "And I'm sure Lulu can't eat all that."

"Certainly she can. Why not? You starved the poor tyke all day yesterday."

Flora returned to her newspaper. Presently she looked up. "When are you leaving?"

"Right after breakfast." The talk continued. Lulu gathered that Maurice would be gone several days on a business trip, in connection with buying some land.

The boys came downstairs, and received sharp reprimands from Maurice. They ignored Lulu, quarreled over the funnypapers, so stridently that Maurice reached over, took the papers from both of them. "Now let's have some peace and quiet."

Maurice departed shortly after breakfast, and a few minutes later Kendall started to saunter from the house.

Flora, who seemed to have the all-seeing eyes of Argus, called him back. "Just where are you going?"

Kendall scowled over his shoulder. "Good heavens, do I have to fill out time-tables every time I walk down the street?"

"That's quite enough of your impudence, young man. While you're living in this house, you'll conduct yourself by our rules, not your own."

"I was just going down to the Virdens'," growled Kendall.

"Well, I have a little job for you and Oliver; with Giorgio's help, I want you to bring the old oak chiffonier up from the basement."

"That old monster? Good heavens, that's a job for about four stevedores!"

"You three can handle it quite easily; it's not as heavy as all that. We'll just bring it up right now."

With Flora supervising, Kendall, Oliver and the house-boy tugged, strained, heaved, hauled, and finally delivered the bureau into Lulu's room. Lulu had wanted to help but Oliver growled at her and Kendall told her to keep out of the way, so while the bureau was shoved into place against the wall she sat on the bed, legs tucked tidily beneath her.

"There," said Flora, "a nice dresser for all your things. It needs a good dusting of course, and you had better put fresh lining in all the drawers."

Lulu approached the old bureau without enthusiasm. It smelled of the basement, and the brown oak looked dingy beside the oystershell enamel of the other furniture.

Flora smiled faintly, then turned and left the room. Lulu found a dust-rag, conscientiously wiped the sour old varnish, laid newspapers in the drawers, and put away her clothes. To her mild surprise Flora offered no further advice, criticism or comment, and seemed to have forgotten all about her. As a matter of fact Flora was dressing for a Theosophical Society tea, and had no time to spare. Lulu finished at just about the same time Flora was ready to depart, and watched Flora sweep down the stairs dressed in an elegant dove-gray suit, with a silver-gray fox-fur around her neck.

Oliver had the misfortune to appear from the kitchen eating a peanut-butter sandwich. Flora wrinkled her nose in disgust. "Oliver, you simply must stop this eating between meals; you're becoming repulsively fat."

"I haven't had anything to eat since breakfast!" cried Oliver indignantly. "I'm hungry!"

"Never mind all that," said Flora. "Please don't contradict me. And you may take Lulu down the street to the Robinsons', and introduce her to Mary and Celia."

Oliver's jaw relaxed, his mouth opened in incredulous dismay. "*Me*? Take her to the Robinsons'?"

"You heard me perfectly well."

"Oh *rats*!"

"That will be quite enough from you, young man." Flora gave him a last monitory glance and swept out the door. Oliver followed making plaintive outcries which Flora ignored.

For fifteen minutes Oliver mooched sulkily back and forth in front of the house, then flung himself indoors, called Lulu with the worst possible grace and escorted her up the street.

The Robinson girls were shy, quiet and well-behaved; Lulu spent a pleasant afternoon. At dinner-time Flora sat lost in thought, while Kendall and Oliver ate moodily; Lulu was ignored. As she went to bed she told herself that perhaps things weren't going to be so bad after all.

A week passed; two weeks. The school term was so nearly ended that Lulu stayed at home, with little to do except read, play with the Robinson girls after school, and pull weeds in the back yard. Every day she watched for Chick but he never appeared, nor did she glimpse his face in the upstairs window. Purr, the black kitten, had become wary of the Brewer yard, and Lulu thought it best not to coax him over the fence.

All in all the time passed tolerably. The boys kept their distance, and Aunt Flora almost seemed to forget her existence. Uncle Maurice of course was quite friendly and even playful when Aunt Flora was out of the way — sometimes to an extent which rather puzzled Lulu. One evening indeed he came home flushed and cheerful and smelling of whiskey, and met Lulu coming down the stairs. "My little pal Lulu!" chirruped Maurice. He caught her, lofted her up in his arms, and while Lulu giggled nervously, he turned her over so that her dress fell over her head, then cradling her, nipped at her bare belly.

Lulu squeaked in embarrassment, squirmed, struggled, clutched at her dress, doubled up her knees. Maurice's grip suddenly relaxed, Lulu gained her feet. At the top of the stairs stood Flora, watching with pinched mouth and tilted nose. "You seem in quite good spirits, Maurice," said Flora in her most crystalline voice, "but I'm sure you have embarrassed Lulu. You forget that she is — no longer an infant. I assume you forget."

"Pooh," muttered Maurice. "Bah." He trudged up the stairs, went into his bedroom. Flora drifted quietly after him, and for half an hour the sound of their voices drifted out through the closed door. Three times Maurice opened the door, but pausing in the doorway to make a final retort, would be caught up by a counter-remark and step back to renew the discussion.

Lulu meanwhile sat uncomfortably in the living room, the skin of her stomach still twitching to the recollection of munching teeth.

Maurice at last stalked out of the bedroom, followed by Flora, stiff as a wasp. Maurice went to stand by the window and broodingly survey the bay. Lulu, looking timorously from one to the other, met Flora's gaze, to stare like a hypnotized bird. Flora swung away, and down the stairs. Lulu looked after her. "She hates me," Lulu said with silently moving lips. "She *hates* me!"

For several days Lulu made herself as small as possible. Then one morning, when the sun struck down into the backyard of the house below, Chick reappeared. Lulu ran down to the fence and called with great excitement. "Chick, you're back!"

"Yes," said Chick in a gruff voice. "I'm back."

"Where have you been?"

"In the hospital."

"Ooh!" said Lulu. "What did they do?"

"Lots of things."

"And you're better now?" Lulu asked the question from politeness; she already had a sick certainty what the answer must be, for Professor Chickweed looked as pale as one of the blank pages in his Book of Dreams.

"I guess I'm better," he said carelessly. "At least they didn't say I was worse."

"I hope you get well real soon," said Lulu. "Do you know why?"

"No."

"Because I want to go down to the Marina — especially where all the boats are. I can't go alone and I don't want to go with Kendall or Oliver. They wouldn't take me anyway."

Chick gave her a dour side-glance. "How do you know I'd take you? I don't like girls."

"Oh, Chick. You don't mean that. Do you?"

"Yes. I certainly do."

Lulu looked silently through the fence, her feelings wounded. Chick said airily, "You're not so bad. I like you pretty well. I kinda want to go down to the yacht harbor myself. When I get well. I like boats."

"I do too." Lulu looked over her shoulder, then clambered across the fence. "Here I am!"

"Yeah," said Chick.

Lulu sat down at the table. "Let me look at your book."

"No sir." Chick closed the book with a decisive snap.

"My, you're bashful!"

"I'm no such thing."

"Tell me about the hospital."

Chick shrugged his frail shoulders. "There's nothing to tell."

"Was it nice there?"

"Oh — it's all right. But I don't like it. There's too many sick people. About half of 'em die, and they wheel 'em out during the night so nobody sees them all."

"Ooh!" said Lulu, her mouth pursed into an O. "Did you see them?"

"No. I didn't look … It scares me, a little." Chick looked fretfully over his shoulder.

"What's the trouble?"

"I'm cold. Don't you think it's cold out here?"

Lulu pursed her lips. "Well — I guess it's pretty cold."

"I'm going inside." Chick hoisted himself to his feet, looked around the yard, everywhere but at Lulu. "You can come in, if you want to."

"All right." Lulu turned a quick glance up to the back of the Brewer house, but no one seemed to be watching. With an unfamiliar and uncomfortable sense of guilt she followed Chick into the house.

They passed through a kitchen into a hall, which led to a foyer; and, beyond, a living room furnished with a green overstuffed couch, a pair of matching armchairs and a television set. The house seemed to be vacant except for Chick and Lulu. "Where's your father and mother?" asked Lulu.

"My father works," said Chick in an offhand voice. "He runs a garage." He added carelessly, "My mother's divorced. She lives in Reno. Come on, I'll take you up to my room."

With an exciting sense of doing something she was sure would be frowned on Lulu followed Chick up the stairs. He moved slowly and Lulu looked down at the stairs to avoid the sight of his corn-stalk ankles.

Chick paused at a door. "This," he said, "is my room." And he swung the door wide. "Enter."

Lulu, now rather nervous, walked in ahead of Chick. She stopped short, totally unprepared for the intricacy and diversity which confronted her.

It was clear that Chick had an active and methodical mind, with a tendency toward the bizarre. On the bed sprawled Purr, sound asleep. A card-table supported an intricate contrivance built from an Erector set. "That's a double merry-go-round," Chick explained. "The bottom turns one way, the top goes the other." One wall displayed several hundred small photographs. "Baseball players," said Chick. Over the bed hung a plywood panel painted with a dozen colors in a curious design of circles, triangles and odd words. "That's a magic symbol," said Chick, "in case I want to call up some evil spirits." On another wall hung a National Geographic map of the world, stuck in various sectors with pins. "Those are where my pen-pals live," said Chick. "I write sometimes ten letters a week." Against another wall leaned or hung an astonishing assortment of sporting equipment: a football helmet, a bat and a mitt, a pair of skis, fishing tackle, a .22 rifle, a set of swim fins with a snorkel, a tennis racket. Chick made a disparaging gesture. "My father buys me those things. He thinks I'll want to get well sooner."

"Do you?" asked Lulu, rather foolishly, as she instantly realized.

Chick answered seriously. "No. I'm not interested in sports, not too much. My father thinks I ought to be and I can't put all this stuff in a closet... If I did he'd think I was getting worse. If I ever get well — when I get well — I'm going to give all those things away. To poor people."

Lulu looked at his book-case. "My, you have lots of books," she said admiringly. "Have you read them all?"

"Naturally." He picked out a worn volume. "Here's *The Mysterious Island*, by Jules Verne. Have you ever read it?"

"No. What's it about?"

"Oh — some men get stranded on an island and have a lot of adventures. I've got all of Edgar Rice Burroughs, everything he wrote... Do you play chess?"

"Not very well. I played with my father, but he always beat me."

"I play chess by mail. I've got three games going. This one here —" he pointed to a small board set up with chessmen "— this has been going for over six months."

"That must be fun," said Lulu dutifully.

"Uh-huh. I'll show you my designs." He hesitated. "Promise on your word of honor you'll never tell anybody if I show you something?"

"I promise. I really do."

Chick nodded. "Okay. Look." He went to the wall, which was paneled with plywood, pushed at a certain spot. The plywood bent in, to reveal a dark gap. "It's my secret hiding place," said Chick. "I keep my designs and my Book of Dreams in here." He reached in and withdrew a loose-leaf binder, which he brought to the desk. He opened it reverently, and Lulu bent forward with interest. She leaned against

Chick, and became uneasily conscious of a faint unpleasant odor, compounded of hospital antiseptic and unhealthy flesh. Chick turned a page. "Ooh," said Lulu, "that's pretty."

Chick turned page after page, each of which displayed an intricate geometrical design he had constructed with ruler and compass and colored with poster-paints.

The showing completed, Chick put the folder back in his hiding place, and tucked the Book of Dreams in after.

Lulu asked, "Do you just write down dreams and nothing else?"

"No," said Chick. "I write lots of things. When something important happens I write it down." He paused, looked out the window. "When you came, I wrote it down."

Lulu became flamingly embarrassed, and Chick's white ears were visited with a tinge of pink. Lulu said vaguely, "I guess I better get back, Aunt Flora will be worried about me." With her fantastic honesty she was forced to qualify, "At least she'll be wondering where I am."

"Hmmf," growled Chick. "Are you going to tell?"

"Tell what?"

"About my room? And my hiding place?"

Lulu felt a momentary twinge of anger. "I promised I wouldn't."

"I know. Most people don't keep their promises."

Lulu looked at him doubtfully, frowned. This was a new idea to her; she had assumed that promises were universally binding, on pain of something unusual and rather awful. "I guess I better go. It's almost time for lunch."

Chick nodded dourly. "Maybe I'll see you tomorrow."

"Maybe." Lulu left the room, descended the stairs, went out the back door. As she crossed the yard she looked up to see Chick watching her, his eyes black and glowing with — for want of a better expression — dark radiance. "Poor Chick," said Lulu. "Poor Chick … He can't die, when he likes to live so much …"

She climbed the fence and returned to the Brewer house, uneasy lest someone show an interest in where she had spent her morning. But her Uncle Maurice was downtown and her Aunt Flora seemed to have other affairs on her mind.

＊

"Kendall," said Nancy, "I've got to talk to you."

"Go ahead," said Kendall. "Talk."

"Not here. Let's go out into the court."

Unwillingly Kendall accompanied her along the corridor, out into a sunny paved court between the school and the gymnasium. She stopped, turned, faced him. Kendall thought she looked rather clenched and wan.

"I'm pregnant."

"What!" Kendall threw his head back, surveyed her with wonder. Then the full impact of the statement struck him. "You don't mean —"

"Yes. You."

Kendall felt somehow foolish and ineffectual. "That's — a weird thing to have happen," he said with a ghastly attempt at humor.

Nancy blurted, "We've got to get married."

"What!"

"Yes."

"But … I mean — well, are you sure?"

"I missed my period. I never did before. And I've been sick to my stomach."

"This is awful," said Kendall bleakly.

"Yes."

"Can't you get rid of it?"

Nancy shook her head. "That's a sin. It's murder."

Kendall's eyes went to the crucifix she wore around her neck. "Rats. You don't believe all that stuff."

"Yes," she whispered. "I do believe it. It's a sin…"

"I can't get married," said Kendall roughly. "That's crazy!"

"We've got to. We've simply got to."

This was Friday afternoon.

Chapter VII

After lunch on Saturday Lulu found herself alone in the house. Kendall and Oliver were off somewhere on business of their own. Maurice had a business engagement which (so Lulu gathered from breakfast conversation) would almost certainly result in a tremendous profit. Maurice had spoken largely of a summer in Europe, Flora was reminded of a set of antique oriental rugs just arrived at Gumps, and which she would investigate this very day. So Lulu, sitting alone at the big walnut dining room table, was served a sandwich, a bowl of soup and a glass of milk by the house-boy.

After lunch she went upstairs and looked out across the garden. But the yard across the fence was vacant and Chick's window showed only as a dark gap.

Lulu went into her room, and from boredom, combed out her hair, brushed it, tied it with a black ribbon.

She liked the effect so much that she changed into a knitted white blouse and a dark blue skirt. Then, feeling very much a young lady, went out into the sitting-room, kneeled on the couch, and pressed her nose to the back window.

The front door opened, thudded shut. From below came the whistled phrase with which Maurice was wont to announce his presence in the house. Lulu felt a sudden little qualm of uneasiness. She turned her head, listened as Maurice mounted the stairs, half of a mind to run into her room. Too late. He came up into the hall, looked into the sitting-room, saw her. His face was pink and cheerful; he swayed slightly. Lulu recognized the signs. Uncle Maurice had enjoyed a convivial lunch.

"Well, well," called Maurice. "It's my little pal, and my my, doesn't she look pretty today? Regular little movie starlet." He crossed the room, sat down beside her. "And how's everything going with my little Lulu?"

"All right," said Lulu primly. She twisted around, slid off the couch, but Maurice caught her around the waist, pulled her back across his lap. Lulu pulled her skirt down over her knees.

"Do you know what happened this morning?" said Maurice in a low chuckling voice. "Your buddy-buddy cleaned up. Money? What's money? We can throw it away. Do you know what he's going to buy you?"

"No," said Lulu, fascinated in spite of herself.

"How would you like — a lovely horse, of your very own?"

"Ooh!" said Lulu. "I'd like it. I like horses. Where would I ride him?"

"In the park. Anywhere. Up and down the street. Up the stairs into your room."

Lulu giggled. "Aunt Flora wouldn't let me."

Maurice stroked her face, settled her more comfortably. He said in a jocular voice, "You know what Aunt Flora can do?"

"No."

"Aunt Flora can go chase herself." Maurice looked up in mock alarm. "But don't tell her I said so."

"I won't."

"Good. It's a secret. Between just you and me."

"All right."

"I'm waiting," said Maurice.

"For what?" Lulu wriggled herself slightly around.

"For a kiss. Isn't a horse — a lovely black horse with beautiful saddle — worth a kiss?"

"I don't have the horse yet," said Lulu saucily.

Maurice groaned. "You women are all alike. Here! Where are you going?"

"I'm leaving," said Lulu. "I'll sit in the chair."

"Bah," said Maurice. "I've held dozens of girls in my lap, most of them heavier than you. And you know the game we always played?"

"No."

— 61 —

"It's like this. You see my hand? You catch it before it catches you. Ready — set — go!" He gave Lulu's nose a tweak. "Ha, ha! You missed. Now. Try again. Ready — set — go!" Lulu grasped, but Maurice eluded her and caught the calf of her leg. Lulu laughed nervously. "You tickle."

"Not really. Now. Ready — set — go!" Lulu grasped, Maurice's hand went under her skirt and caught her in the most *astonishing* place. Lulu sat shocked and stiff. And there standing on the stairs was Oliver; she saw his smirking face.

Lulu tugged at Maurice's hand. "Don't, don't *do* that."

"That's part of the game," said Maurice.

Lulu became frantic; she started to cry. "Don't, please don't, I'll tell Aunt Flora if you don't stop!"

Maurice's face changed instantly. His body became rigid, he drew away from her. Lulu stole a glance at him and was frightened by the way his eyelids slanted across his eyes. Maurice said softly, "So that's the way it is, eh? And all this time I've stuck up for you, been your buddy!"

"I don't want to — to be tickled. Like that. I don't like it." Tears came to Lulu's eyes, her face crinkled, she sat perched rigidly on the points of Maurice's knees, desperately wanting to get down, but afraid to move.

"Very well," said Maurice, with an awful note of finality in his voice. "Then that's the way it is. We're not buddy-buddies any more." He pushed her off his lap, sat stonily watching her. Lulu stood for a moment sobbing, her hands to her face, then turned and ran blindly to her room.

Maurice sighed, muttered, blew his breath gustily out between his teeth, rose to his feet, and with a clenched jaw stared out over the bay.

Kendall could hardly have chosen a more unfortunate time to bring his own bad news. Maurice listened with a sour half-grin, nodding from time to time. Kendall finished, peered hopefully up into Maurice's face.

Maurice nodded once or twice more. "Well, my boy, it looks like you're caught."

"Caught?" croaked Kendall.

"Certainly. There's only one honorable thing to do — so do it."

"I don't know what you mean," faltered Kendall.

"Don't know what 'honor' means? It's perfectly simple. You've made your bed, you've got to lie in it."

Kendall's eyes bulged in desperation. "But — it's silly! Me — married!"

"Yes," said Maurice. "It is silly. And it's pretty silly you helling around at night and putting your dingus places it don't belong."

Kendall swung away. He went up into his room until Flora came home, then he came downstairs, took her aside and spilled his burden of grief.

Flora stood cool and still and remote. She laughed. "It's ridiculous, of course."

Kendall felt a great weight leave him. "Then I don't have to marry her?"

"It's obviously impossible. She's as much to blame as you are, and she'll simply have to take the consequences."

"Father said —"

"I don't care what your father said. I wouldn't even consider having you married."

Maurice's voice came heavy and harsh. "You don't have any voice in the matter. I say he's going to do the right thing, whether you lose one of your precious boys or not."

Flora shrugged, turned away. "I don't care to discuss it."

Maurice returned to the living room, Flora went upstairs with Kendall and had a long talk. Oliver lay on his bed, eyes liquid with excitement.

"Your father," said Flora, "is an obstinate man, as you know. He has his own faults, yet he refuses to understand someone else's weaknesses."

Oliver leaned forward, his mouth quivering. "You know what I saw today when I came home?"

Flora listened, but pretended to pooh-pooh the whole matter. "I'm sure your eyes were deceiving you, Oliver. And it's not nice to spread tales of this kind."

"I saw it!" cried Oliver. "I was standing right at the head of the stairs. She was sitting on his lap laughing."

Flora nodded. "I have no doubt she's a sly little bit, but — well, you're still too young to understand. Both of you forget all this, do you understand? Forget it, through and through. It's disgraceful that you'd even consider talking about your father like this."

Flora went downstairs. Maurice sat in his leather arm-chair, furiously smoking his pipe and reading the newspaper.

Flora went to stand in front of him. "Maurice."

Maurice looked up at her. "Yes?"

"Just what was going on here this afternoon?"

Maurice blinked. "Why do you ask?"

Flora laughed. "Oliver has a very odd story to tell. He seems to believe that — I really find it hard to put into words. And I can't believe that Lulu is — quite so precocious."

She turned, swept away. Maurice sat like a statue, his pipe held at an odd angle. He rose suddenly to his feet, stalked upstairs, into the boys' bedroom.

Kendall sat limply in a chair, Oliver lay on his bed, eating an apple. Maurice stalked up to him, knocked the apple from his hand, cuffed him, flung him to the floor. Oliver stared up uncomprehendingly. "Rotten little sneak," said Maurice. "I'm not forgetting this." He looked at the table beside Oliver's bed, picked up a box of peanut brittle. Maurice nodded. "For one thing you're going to cut down on the sweets. Entirely. Don't let me catch you with candy." He turned to Kendall.

"Come along, Kendall."

Kendall looked up. "Where?"

"Never mind where. Come along."

With lagging steps and despairing glances over his shoulder, Kendall followed Maurice downstairs, out the front door.

They got into the car. Flora flung open the bedroom window, called down in a carefully modulated voice, "Oh, Maurice! Just where are you going?"

Maurice made no answer. The Lincoln swung off down the street. "Where does this girl live?" he demanded.

Kendall told him in a listless voice.

Flora went into Lulu's room. Lulu looked up with a tearstained face. Flora looked down. In a sugar-sweet voice she said, "You are a very depraved little girl. I don't know what will become of you — but I can well imagine."

She swung out of the room. Lulu uncomprehendingly watched the door close.

Maurice rang the bell in vain. No one answered. He and the hang-dog Kendall returned to the car, drove home. When they walked into the house Flora swept forward. "Where have you been? Tell me, where have you been?"

"Out to get a marriage license," said Maurice. "The girl, however, was not at home. Tomorrow or Monday will do as well."

"Don't you think you are acting rather impulsively?" she asked gently. "After all, only a month has passed. The girl may not even be pregnant, and you'd be making a fool of yourself."

Maurice marched upstairs. "We shall see."

The dinner gong sounded. Lulu huddled more closely against the bed than ever. A minute or so passed. Leaden footsteps sounded in the hall. Kendall? Oliver? Lulu stirred uneasily. She slowly sat up, swung her legs over the edge of the bed. Her hair was mussed, her eyes were swollen. She had better go down: sometime she'd have to leave the room... In a sudden spasm of indignation she jumped to her feet. "I haven't done anything, so I don't need to be ashamed!" So she scolded herself. "It's silly for me to be hiding in here."

She combed her hair and marched defiantly out of the room and down the stairs. As she approached the dining room her heart sank and her steps faltered. But as she slipped into her seat only Oliver looked at her — a sidewise glance, sly and inquiring. Lulu raised her eyebrows to convey contempt and disdain.

Dinner was silent and grim; Lulu was glad she had come down: she would have been more conspicuous otherwise.

Dessert was served — a chocolate cake with whipped cream. Oliver stole a glance toward Maurice, who watched sternly while Flora cut the cake. She served Oliver; Maurice reached out, removed the plate. Oliver's face puckered in distress.

"No more desserts for you," said Maurice, grinning widely — a grimace more than a smile. "Not till you get rid of that disgusting puppy-fat."

Flora looked at him with narrowed eyes. "Aren't you being rather unreasonable?"

"I've been too easy with all of you," said Maurice harshly. "Things are going to be different from now on."

Flora gave a secret bitter little chuckle, and pushed away her own cake.

Maurice ate slowly, methodically, while Oliver watched with a wide tragic gaze. Maurice finished. "You may be excused," he said, but now in his voice a faint hollow note of pomposity could be detected, and it vitiated the entire effect of his previous harshness. Maurice sensed the let-down himself. He glared around the table. "I said you may be excused!"

"Please don't shout, Maurice," said Flora. "We'll leave the table when we are quite ready."

Maurice jumped up and left the table himself. As soon as he had left the room, Flora with great dignity served Oliver his cake. But Maurice almost on cue returned, swept the cake to the side, swung Oliver's chair away from the table. "That's all. Don't let me catch you in a trick like that again."

Oliver slunk out of the room, Flora swept after him.

Lulu went directly to bed, but lay staring sleeplessly up into the dark.

Sunday morning breakfast was only a trifle more relaxed. Oliver protested when Maurice stopped him from sugaring his grapefruit. "I can't eat it sour."

"You certainly can, and what's more you will."

Flora said coolly, "I wish you'd stop bullying the poor child."

Maurice shifted in his chair, surveyed Oliver. "Poor little sneak."

Flora addressed herself to her own grapefruit. Presently she said, "We've got to come to some decision on this other matter."

Maurice looked up, instantly truculent. "What other matter?"

Flora gave a knowing little sniff. "Kendall's difficulties."

"That matter is out of our hands."

"Don't be ridiculous, Maurice. These things are arranged all the time, as I'm sure you're aware."

"She's a Catholic," growled Kendall. "She'd never have an operation."

Flora said cuttingly, "You know far too much about matters which you shouldn't be at all interested in."

Maurice leaned disgustedly back in his chair. "For heaven's sake, Flora, you're living in the twentieth century."

Flora paid no attention to him. "We know nothing about the girl, or her family; she's probably just a little tramp."

Kendall protested feebly, "She's really a very nice girl."

"In that case there's no more to be said." Maurice rose to his feet. "I think we'd better plan to visit the girl and talk the matter over with her family." He turned Lulu a glance cold as the gaze of a fish, and left the room.

Now he hates me, thought Lulu. They all hate me. But I don't care.

Flora sipped her cup of tea, while Kendall morosely moved a spoon back and forth on the tablecloth.

Flora said, "I'm afraid your father has made up his mind to be obstinate. In which case —" she shrugged her shoulders.

Kendall looked up as if he had been betrayed. "Do you mean —"

"I don't mean anything. Except that we'll have to wait and see."

"He'll make me get married."

Flora said with sudden spite, "And it will serve you right." She left the room. Kendall glared at Lulu. "What are you looking at?"

"Nothing." With great dignity Lulu rose and likewise left the room, leaving Kendall to brood over his misfortunes.

Lulu went out into the back garden. The sky was blue, the sun shone brightly, sparrows twittered in the maple tree. The world was a different place.

Behind Chick's bedroom window a face flickered, and a few minutes later Chick came out into his yard, wearing pajamas and a blue bathrobe. After him, sedately marching, came Purr. Chick came to the fence. "Hello."

"Hello," said Lulu. "It's a beautiful day."

"Yes." Chick scrutinized the sky as if to fathom the exact constituents which made the day so exceptional. Lulu thought that Chick himself almost looked beautiful this morning. His pallor contrasted with the black of his hair; the angularity of his features gave strength and energy to the fragile bones which underlaid them. He said, "You look worried."

"Things are simply awful," said Lulu. She looked back up at the house. Kendall and Oliver were looking down from the second-floor living room. Lulu turned haughtily away. "Kendall's going to get married."

Chick's eyebrows rose. "'Married'? What for?"

"I don't know. His girl friend is having a baby, so Kendall is going to marry her." Lulu knit her brows. "I thought only married people had babies." She giggled nervously. "I hope I don't have one."

Chick regarded her sardonically sidewise, but made no comment. He looked up toward the Brewer house and his face darkened. "Here come your cousins. Come here, Purr."

Purr had climbed the maple tree and was scratching his claws in the bark. Chick went to his table and sat down.

Kendall and Oliver ambled down the walk. Kendall threw himself down on the lawn and chewed a blade of grass. Oliver went to the fence, peered through. "Hey, Chickweed."

Chick made no reply.

"Hey!" called Oliver. "Chickweed! Don't you hear me?"

Chick looked up. "What do you want?"

"Nothing. I want to find out if you were deaf." He sat down on the lawn beside Kendall. Lulu abstractedly pulled a dandelion from the pansy bed. "Hey, Chickweed," called Oliver once more, watching Lulu maliciously sidewise.

"What do you want?"

"Be careful with Lulu. If she shows you too good a time it might kill you."

Lulu looked up, blushing furiously. "You better be careful, Oliver."

"I guess we all been missing out, hey Kendall?" crowed Oliver. "C'mon Lulu, put on a strip-tease for us."

"She's too young," said Kendall in a bored voice. "She doesn't have anything."

"You two are disgusting," said Lulu. "You're the two nastiest meanest boys I've ever seen."

Oliver mimicked her: "Oh woop-de-do!...Hey, Kendall! Look at that cat. It's caught a bird."

Kendall raised his head, searched up into the branches. "Throw a rock at it."

Oliver threw a rock, but Purr dodged, crouched, glared down behind his feathery mustache. Chick rose to his feet, peered up into the trees. "Here, Purr, here Purr!"

"That's what your rotten cat does!" shouted Oliver indignantly. "Catches birds!"

"Get the gun," said Kendall lazily. "Shoot it."

Oliver stood poised, entranced with the idea. "Should I?"

"Sure," said Kendall with one eye on Chick. "It's on our property, killing birds. Shoot the damn thing."

"Don't you dare!" shrilled Lulu.

"Don't worry," called Chick through the fence. "They wouldn't dare."

"That's what you think," said Kendall. "Go on, Oliver — get my gun. I'm sick of that damn cat."

Chick called up into the tree. "Here Purr! C'mon down, boy…"

Purr, attending to the bird, ignored him completely.

Oliver came excitedly back from the rear porch with the gun. "Here's the shells."

Kendall, with sinister deliberation, loaded the gun, watching Chick, who had pressed himself against the fence. Kendall called, "Well, Chickweed, once and for all, are you gonna keep that cat out of our garden?"

Chick's mouth opened and closed. "C'mon, Chick," said Kendall ominously. "Let's have an answer." He cocked the gun.

Chick turned, ran waveringly for his house. Kendall laughed, lowered the gun. "Look at him go."

Oliver squinted up at Purr, then back to Kendall. "Aren't you going to shoot him?"

"Go ahead, if you want to," said Kendall. "Nobody told you not to." He leaned back on the lawn.

"Okay," said Oliver. "I will." He reached for the gun, but Lulu darted forward, snatched it away.

"Give that here," barked Oliver, advancing slowly.

"Keep away from me," said Lulu. "Be careful. This gun is loaded."

"Put down that gun," barked Kendall, sitting up. "You damn little fool, it's ready to shoot."

"I know," said Lulu. "But you're not going to hurt Purr!"

Oliver looked up at the back windows of the house; Maurice at this moment sauntered up to the glass. Oliver cupped his hands. "Lulu's pointing the gun at us! And it's loaded!"

"I did not," cried Lulu.

Maurice turned majestically away from the window. Kendall and Oliver turned to look at Lulu. "Now you're going to get it," said Oliver. "Nobody's supposed to point a gun at anyone else."

"I didn't point the gun at you."

"The point was toward me. You had your hand on the trigger."

"I did not."

"It was right at the trigger! I saw it myself!"

Maurice stalked out of the house. "What's all this?" he rasped.

All three spoke at once. "Quiet," said Maurice. He surveyed Lulu with a yellow gleam in his eye, then turned to Oliver. "What happened?"

"Lulu picked up the gun, pointed it at me when I went to take it away from her," said Oliver excitedly. "She had her hand on the trigger —"

Maurice inspected Lulu, and cold chills ran up and down her body. Her knees felt weak, her heart thumped. "I didn't. I didn't!" she wailed.

Maurice smiled. "I saw you myself," he said in a soft voice. He turned to Kendall and Oliver. "Go on into the house."

Kendall and Oliver reluctantly withdrew, looking over their shoulders. Maurice waited till the door closed behind them, then came slowly forward to the paralyzed Lulu. "I'm going to punish you," said Maurice. "So that you'll remember, never, never to point a gun at anybody." He took her arm, turned her over his knee, drew up her skirt, pulled her pants down, spanked her bare bottom. Five times his hand came down, while Lulu lay limp in a paralysis compounded of shock, embarrassment and fear. He pulled her upright, looked down into her face, which was white and pinched and agonized. "I hate you," said Lulu. "I hate you."

"Ah ha," said Maurice. "So that's how it is. Need some more, eh?" Back over his knee, more of the same. Once again he stood her up. "*I hate you!*" gasped Lulu, pulling up her pants.

"Okay. More." Lulu tore herself away. She saw the gun, grabbed it, turned, a small animal at bay. Purr came down from the tree with his bird. Maurice kicked him aside, came forward. "What did I tell you about that gun!"

"Leave me alone," gasped Lulu. "Don't touch me!"

But Maurice stalked forward, magnificent in his wrath. He loomed over her, tall as the trees.

Lulu wailed, a thin wild almost soundless cry. She squinted her eyes closed and off went the gun, with a terrible noise. Her eyes opened wide, to see Maurice reeling back and away. The gun dropped, she turned and ran. A hoarse cry came after her, but she paid no heed. Across the lawn, up the steps, out on the sidewalk, along the street, down the hill. She began to gasp, the breath was hot in her throat, a stitch caught in her side. She faltered, slowed to a staggering trot, a walk. Then she halted, leaned against a telephone pole. Fearfully she looked behind, the way she had come. There was no one in sight. No one had pursued her; she stood alone halfway along a strange block. She sobbed, turned, walked on. She ran a few erratic paces, then once more slowed to a walk. At the corner she stopped, and wondered where she was going. Down the hill gleamed the Sunday morning bay, clean and blue, with sailboats gliding in and out of the yacht harbor. She looked back again. Where to go? What to do? She asked herself the questions, but no answers came. The future was no longer than the next block.

She walked slowly down the hill toward the yacht harbor, and presently came to a long area of lawn. This seemed far enough. She went to a bench, seated herself, and watched others who, like herself, had reason to come down to the Marina this bright Sunday morning. There were boys flying kites, old men walking dogs, trios and quartets of high school girls, persons without definable characteristics or purpose. No one paid any attention to Lulu except a small boy of four or five who asked her to play catch with him. Lulu shook her head.

The afternoon slipped past. A wind began to blow in through the Golden Gate, countering the sun's warmth. When a cloud passed in front of the sun, goosepimples began to form on Lulu's arms... She looked back up the hill. Somewhere in that jumble of roofs and walls and windows was the house were she lived; where Uncle Maurice and Aunt Flora would be waiting for her, where Kendall and Oliver would be sitting awed and oppressed by the dramatic enormity of Lulu's conduct. She had shot a gun at Uncle Maurice. And Lulu wondered what would be done to her. Another spanking? All the rest of the day in her room and no dinner? Lulu blinked nervously. She didn't want to go home. But there was no other place to go.

The wind was blowing quite freshly now and the bay was rimed with white-caps. The sunlight suddenly faded; Lulu looked up with a shiver; she had no idea the sun had dropped so low: it had become a pallid near-invisible disk behind a wall of fog thrusting in through the Golden Gate.

Lulu rose to her feet, hugging herself. She was cold; she had better go home and face the music…Where, exactly, was home? Somewhere up that hill…Lulu sat back on the bench, stared unseeingly at the bay. The truth was, she did not want to go home. But she had to; she had to go somewhere…Out on Marina Boulevard the door of a parked car opened; a man came out, walked toward Lulu, stood over her. She looked up, heart suddenly in her mouth: it was a policeman.

But he seemed amiable enough. He said, "Hello there, young lady."

"Hello," Lulu responded weakly.

"You've been sitting here a long time. Aren't you getting cold?"

Lulu considered. She nodded judiciously. "I am kind of cold."

"Why don't you go home?"

Lulu looked thoughtfully up the hill, not knowing quite how to explain the situation. "I guess I'll go now."

"That's a good idea," said the policeman. "It's getting late and your mother will be worried. Where do you live?"

"Up the hill. On Belvedere Street."

"That's a long way," said the policeman. "You came down here all by yourself?"

"Yes. I walked."

"Well, we'd better give you a ride home. Come along."

Lulu followed, and got in the front seat.

"What's the address?" asked the policeman.

"2413 Belvedere Street."

She wondered what Aunt Flora and Uncle Maurice would think when she arrived home in the police car. Would they be impressed? Or annoyed? She was too tired and miserable to care.

They drove up the hill. The policeman was very handsome, thought Lulu, and not too old — rather like the hero in a Western movie. He looked at her occasionally as he drove, and presently he asked, "Does your mother know you went for a walk?"

"My mother is dead," said Lulu. "I live with Aunt Flora and Uncle Maurice."

"Oh. I see. And they know where you are?"

"No." Lulu stole a glance at the policeman. He seemed polite and rather kind. She wondered what would happen if...It all came out in a rush. "I really don't want to go home, I really don't. Could I come live with you? Please let me."

He laughed, in not too much surprise. "That would be very nice; but I don't think your aunt and uncle would allow it."

"Yes they would," said Lulu. "They don't like me. Especially after today." She fell abruptly silent.

"What happened today?"

Tears began to trickle down Lulu's cheeks. "Uncle Maurice spanked me."

"That's nothing. Everybody gets a spanking when they're bad."

"But I wasn't bad. Kendall and Oliver said I pointed the gun at them, but I really didn't. Uncle Maurice came down, and I told him but he wouldn't listen."

"Well, well, well!" said the policeman.

Lulu reflected. The policeman seemed very nice. It might be a good idea to explain things to him, and perhaps he'd be on her side when they got home — perhaps even try to make Aunt Flora understand things... She spoke, as casually as she was able, but her voice trembled a bit. "When Uncle Maurice spanked me — the gun went off. I don't think I hurt him, I don't think he was hurt..."

"Well, well, well!"

"I was scared. He was acting —" Lulu screwed up her eyes "— kind of funny. He scared me. I didn't mean to, well, shoot the gun."

"So," said the policeman. "You think you might have shot your uncle?"

"Not really," said Lulu. "I don't think so."

"You don't know?"

"No. I ran away. I ran down to the yacht harbor."

"Well!" said the policeman. He turned the car into a familiar block, drew up in front of the Brewer house. It was already dark, and lights shone yellow through all the windows. "Here we are. Is that your house?"

"Yes." Lulu made no move to open the door. She really didn't want to go inside. She looked at the policeman. "Do I have to go in?"

"Oh yes," said the policeman. He seemed just a trifle less friendly. "We've got to find out what's happened since you've been gone." He got out of the car, walked around the front, opened the door for her. "Come along."

Lulu reluctantly got out. He took her hand, they marched up the walk, up the steps, along the vestibule to the door. Lulu thought that the house seemed unusually bright, as if every light in the house were switched on. The policeman rang the doorbell.

Footsteps within — quick wild footsteps. The door opened; Flora stood looking out. She wore some kind of loose white robe; her eyes were wide; the whites showed completely around the pupils; her hair hung disheveled around her neck. In all her later life, when Lulu remembered this confrontation, and when her stock of associations had been tremendously augmented, the name 'Medea' came instantly to her mind. Medea, Medea — Medea stood in the doorway, eyes blazing, hair in disarray. From the policeman she looked to Lulu. "So," she said in a rasping uneven voice, "you decided to come back."

The policeman asked sharply, "Is there some trouble, ma'am?"

Flora raised her hands, the fingers trembled. "Trouble?" She leaned forward, swaying over Lulu who shrank back. "Trouble? Ha ha! Look at her, the evil imp!"

The policeman glanced down at Lulu, who began to whimper. "I'm afraid I don't understand."

"Ask her! But take her away, before I do something terrible."

"I'm sorry, ma'am, but will you please tell me what's happened?"

Flora became rigid, her arm at the doorknob, supporting her body like a buttress. "She shot my husband. He's dead. She killed him, the evil little creature — the finest man Heaven ever put on this earth." And Flora transfixed Lulu with a gaze like the stab of a dagger. "She came into my house —"

"Excuse me, ma'am, but you naturally called a doctor?"

"— and now Maurice is gone, dead. Forever. Take her away," cried Flora in a grating crow-voiced screech. "Take her away!"

"Yes ma'am," said the policeman stiffly. "But first I must make sure that you called a doctor."

"Yes, yes, yes. Dr. Knapp." Flora leaned against the door, closed it. Through the small curtained pane the policeman saw her reel away toward the stairs, mount them with limp mindless motions. The policeman shrugged. A very emotional woman. He glanced dubiously down at Lulu who stood rigid, taut-faced, against the wall. Evil imp? The policeman reserved judgment — which in any event would not be his to make.

"Come along," he said to Lulu. "We'll have to take you somewhere else."

Lulu followed without question. In the car he called headquarters, made a verbal report, received instructions.

They sat and waited in the dark blue evening. Lulu said nervously, "Are you going to arrest me?"

"No," said the policeman. "Nothing like that. We'll take you to Juvenile Hall and a nice lady will look after you." He eyed her appraisingly. "Why did you shoot him? Was he — doing something you didn't like?"

"He was spanking me," said Lulu in a dull voice. "I was scared — I didn't mean to hurt him... Is he — dead? Really dead?"

"Apparently."

Lulu gasped, as if for the first time she apprehended what had occurred, and began to tremble.

A pair of squad cars pulled up in front of them; there was a brief conference, then the policeman drove Lulu away from the house on Belvedere Street, which she would not see again until many years had passed.

Chapter VIII

Lulu was held at Juvenile Hall for three and a half months, a stay of unusual duration occasioned by the unusual nature of Lulu's situation. Spring became summer and summer passed by. Lulu was examined, interviewed, diagnosed, and analyzed by an assortment of functionaries: talking masks without real existence. Lulu observed them with detachment, responded to their questions — when she understood them — with candor and simplicity. She carried away from the entire duration of her stay only a confused recollection, disconnected images, bright but stark as if seen by the light of a flash-bulb: the hushed dormitory, the long corridors dwindling in surrealistic perspective, the matrons with remote faces and alert eyes. There was a constant flux of children, coming and going, a process fraught with mysterious drama which fascinated and vaguely terrified Lulu. In from the chaos of the outer world came the small wan faces, to stay a few days, a week, a month, and presently to disappear, never to be seen again.

The authorities were in something of a quandary as to what to do with Lulu. Would-be foster parents quickly lost interest: "And that charming little girl — isn't she rather quiet?"

"Oh, indeed, intensely so. I'm sorry to say we can't get much response from her."

"You mean that she's well, slow? Deficient?"

"No. Not really. She's an isolate, as we call them. Oddly enough, this little girl has a rather frightening history of violence."

"Why that's hard to believe! She seems — absolutely angelic."

"Ummf. She shot and killed her uncle, and not long before clubbed her little cousin with a piece of timber."

"Good heavens, that can't be true."

"It is, however."

"Was the uncle — you know — molesting her? I've heard that in cases of this kind —"

"Nothing like that. We'd know where we stood if this were the case. She pointed a gun at her cousins, her uncle punished her and she took the same gun and shot him."

"My, my! To think of all that going on behind such a pretty little face!" And the group would move on.

Flora came to the hall about a week after Lulu's arrival. Not at all anxious to see her aunt, Lulu went reluctantly to the visiting room. Flora's eyes were hard as stone. "Well, Lulu, how are you?"

"I'm all right."

"Do you like it here?" Flora spoke softly, watching Lulu like a hawk.

Lulu reflected a second, and capsulized an entire universe of emotions: "It's all right, I guess."

Flora gave her head a minatory shake. "You realize that you did a terrible thing? I hope that they've explained that to you." Her voice rose a half-octave. "A terrible thing! Now you are being punished. If you were older something quite awful would happen to you."

"I didn't mean to do anything," said Lulu in a low composed voice, and Flora seemed to become even angrier.

"That is quite beside the point. If you —"

"How is Chick?"

"Chick! The little sick boy? I'm sure I don't know."

Lulu moistened her lips. "Is he dead?"

"I know nothing whatever about him." Flora rose to her feet. "You understand that you can't possibly come back to live with us?"

"I don't want to," said Lulu under her breath.

"What was that?" demanded Flora, leaning forward. Lulu maintained silence.

Flora continued frostily. "The authorities will find you a suitable home, and I'll send along your clothes."

Lulu sat looking down at her knees.

"Your Uncle Maurice was to have taken us all abroad this summer," said Flora sibilantly. "Now he's dead and we've lost a great deal of money."

Summer faded into autumn; Lulu was transferred to the State Home for Girls near Santa Rosa. Further months passed, and years, and years added to years. Lulu lived passively, bewildered rather than unhappy, though inevitably she knew many hours of woe. She became familiar with a whole host of odd matters, with extreme states of behavior, with mires and morasses of personality astonishing to find among human beings of any age. The idea of total commitment as an instrument of strategy became familiar to her and undoubtedly shaped her outlook on life, though Lulu herself made no friends and stayed severely aloof from the gangs and cliques which infested the institution.

This fastidiousness made life none the easier. She was called 'stuck-up' and 'conceited', and at the age of eleven was ritualistically beaten up by a group of larger girls.

Nevertheless life continued. Lulu lost her childhood, but in some slight measure of compensation found an early self-sufficiency. She read a great deal, applied herself to her schoolwork with fanatic diligence. At the age of sixteen she was allowed to work part-time at a nearby cannery, and at seventeen, assisted by a scholarship, she enrolled at the University of California, severing all connection with the State Home except for weekly reports to the probation officer.

Lulu was now a slender quiet girl with a pensive expression, undoubtedly pretty. She wore her blonde hair short, and dressed perforce in the simplest clothes. She laughed seldom, but often wore a faint half-smile, which some thought mocking, others quizzical and still others provocative. All agreed, however, that she had a beautiful mouth, sensitive and at once soft and firm. Lulu's voice was clear and quiet; she spoke without emphasis and at first glance seemed polite and conventional — until a sudden gesture, intense, wild, extravagant, hinting of a hundred inner exuberances, completely demolished the illusion. The total effect immensely disturbed the young men of the university, although Lulu never quite took her newly-discovered attraction seriously.

"Lulu," exclaimed one exasperated young man, as they sat parked in front of Lulu's dormitory, "you're absolutely maddening. Why won't you kiss me?"

"Whatever gave you that idea?" said Lulu. She took the young man's head in her hands, kissed his forehead. "There. I kissed you. Aren't you pleased?"

"I'm on the point of becoming violent," groaned the young man. "Don't you like me? Or what?"

"Certainly I like you, Howard. But why get all sweaty?"

"Good Lord!" said Howard. "What kind of a romance is this?"

"I guess…" Lulu paused, while Howard waited. "I guess I'm really not very romantic."

Howard took his arm from around her, slouched down into the seat. "This is too much. Damned if I'm going out with you anymore."

Lulu laughed softly. She opened the door. "If I find I can't stand it I'll telephone you."

"Funny girl," sneered Howard. "Good night." He roared furiously off toward his fraternity house and Lulu forgot all about him.

Her freshman year passed. Her grades were good: three A's and two B's, but failed to satisfy her. She finally pinpointed the cause: her major, which was psychology. It had been selected as a measure of practicality: there were always good jobs available for psychologists. Nevertheless Lulu was uncomfortable. "I don't like this much," she thought, slamming shut her textbook. "But what do I like?" She considered. Business? Economics? Dull. Drab as dishwater. Anthropology? Archaeology? Medicine? Definitely not medicine. Journalism? "I'm not the type," thought Lulu. Art? A possibility. Music? Another possibility. Chemistry? Physics? Mathematics?…Lulu put the idea from her mind. Everything seemed dreary, when what she really wanted to do was ride a bicycle through Europe and explore all the sunny back-regions. Suppose she were a teacher? She'd have every summer free, to travel wherever she chose. But to be a teacher, she must know something to teach. Lulu selected History. During the summer she worked at a Girl Scout Camp, and upon return to Berkeley in the fall changed her major to History. And her sophomore year passed much like her first. Her grades were again excellent; her scholarship was renewed. But again Lulu had qualms about her choice of a career. Suppose she were exiled far out into the desert, or in some unpleasant town in the Central Valley?

During the summer she again worked at the Girl Scout Camp, and one clear evening, walking alone in a meadow, she became entranced by the stars. She thought, why not become an astronomer? When she returned to Berkeley in September she enrolled in Astronomy 1A, to learn if the subject improved on closer acquaintance, or otherwise. Almost at once she decided — otherwise. The textbook looked dry; there was a great deal to do with the optics and mechanics of telescopes, which interested her not at all. The miraculous beauty of the stars themselves was nowhere to be found.

Beside her in the classroom sat a tall somber young man whom she had vaguely noticed around campus the year before. His name was Robert Malloy; he was in his senior year, an electrical engineer specializing in communication. Lulu thought him rather attractive. He was tall, sinewy, if not quite muscular, with dark hair and a clear olive-sallow skin. His nose was high-bridged and Byronic, his jaw tenacious, his eyebrows saturnine, his mouth slanted down at the corners in a manner sometimes melancholy, sometimes droll, sometimes grim. Lulu decided that, rather than an engineer, he seemed a poet or a musician.

Robert Malloy showed only cursory interest in Lulu, which caused her surprise and a certain degree of pique. But gradually as the semester advanced his manner thawed, to the extent that he allowed her a greeting and an occasional dour comment regarding the work of the day.

One morning Lulu spied him on Telegraph Avenue waiting for a traffic signal to change. She decided to cross the street at the same intersection. Their eyes met. "Hello," said Lulu.

"Hello," said Robert Malloy.

They crossed the street. Robert paused, squinted up at the sky, to right and left, then gruffly inquired if Lulu had time for a cup of coffee. Lulu said, yes indeed, it just so happened that she did.

They sat for an hour in a sandwich shop, Lulu doing most of the talking. Robert was not very communicative. He revealed that he had transferred to Cal from N.Y.U. and was of the opinion that anyone who chose to live in New York must be a lunatic. Lulu stated that she'd been born in Japan and had never traveled farther east than — as a matter of fact, she'd never been east at all.

Robert was more relaxed than usual but definitely impersonal. This was one of Lulu's own counters to unwelcome attention. To find it employed against herself was unsettling. She wondered if he were married, and examined his left hand. No ring. A wife and family abandoned in New York? But Robert lacked that almost imperceptible trace of obsequiousness with which marriage brands a man.

The next day in class Robert seated himself beside her with his usual dour nod and ignored her the entire period.

"What an idiot," Lulu told herself, and resolved henceforth to ignore him completely. But after class he approached her and in his most offhand voice asked, "Where do you usually eat lunch?"

"Oh, most anywhere," said Lulu, "when I have money. Toward the end of the month it's crackers and cheese."

Robert scowled off toward the Campanile. "Let's have lunch together."

"Do you mean today? Or tomorrow? Or forever and ever? Because —"

"Yes," said Robert grinning and looking directly down into her face. "Forever and ever and ever."

Lulu saw that she had been mistaken. Robert was definitely not a grouch, nor a boor, nor vacillating, pompous and conceited. Robert was something of a dreamer, she decided, gentle and perhaps even a trifle shy.

They lunched on chili-burgers and milk-shakes, and thereafter met frequently, although always on a casual basis. Robert seemed to like her, and she liked Robert — as much as she could like any human being. She could relax with Robert; he made no demands upon her, and showed only indifference to Lulu's other boy-friends. This latter aspect of their relationship Lulu found somewhat unflattering — especially since he made not even the attempt to hold her hand.

Once or twice they drove up the coast for a Sunday picnic; occasionally he asked her to a movie at one of the little avant-garde theaters surrounding the campus. More often they would meet at the library to study and afterwards drink coffee somewhere along Telegraph Avenue. As the end of the spring semester approached, the knowledge came to Lulu as a shock that Robert was to be graduated, that next year he'd be gone. To her relief she learned that he'd be back as a graduate student. Even if he did treat her like a sister, it was pleasant having him around.

During the summer she worked at Tahoe Tavern as a waitress, and earned considerably more money than she had at the Girl Scout Camp.

Returning to Berkeley in comparative affluence, she rented a two-room apartment to the south of campus. The furniture was rickety, the walls were painted a particularly odious buff, the kitchen was cramped and dark — but for the first time in her life Lulu had a home of her own. She telephoned Robert's old number, doubtful whether or not she'd find him at the same address, but, on the second ring, he answered, almost as if he'd been waiting for her call.

"Robert! It's Lulu."

"Oh. I was just thinking of you."

"I've got an apartment! I'll cook dinner for you. Hamburgers by candle-light. Let me make a list. There's nothing in the house. Hamburger, candles…"

"Let me take you out to dinner instead."

"Actually, that might be easier. Where'll we go?"

"Someplace elegant, in a cheap way. I'll be right over. What's your address?"

She told him; he rang the doorbell twenty minutes later. When she answered the door he held out his hands; it seemed completely natural that she should hug him and kiss him, and both were surprised. Lulu stepped back, laughing and blushing; Robert looked right, left, up and down, and presently said, "I'm glad to see you too."

They drove to San Francisco, dined at a back-street Italian restaurant, wandered aimlessly around North Beach. Lulu was in the best of spirits; she chatted and laughed, then suddenly noticed that Robert had withdrawn into one of his mysterious glooms. She reached out, took his hand. "Robert, have you ever wondered what's going to become of us?"

" 'The cloud-capped towers, the gorgeous palaces, the great globe itself, shall dissolve and leave not a rack behind,' as the Bard puts it. More or less."

"But in the meantime?"

Robert shrugged. "Life is unpredictable. You might marry a saxophonist, or a pastry cook. I might join the Peace Corps. All hell might generally break loose."

"Oh Robert," sighed Lulu, "you're so unsatisfactory sometimes."

Robert grinned sourly. "I'm really very inadequate, in most ways."

Behind the jocularity, Lulu heard an overtone of bitter conviction. She examined him in puzzlement. "What's wrong, Robert?"

"Everything. Mainly myself. But don't worry. It's just an attack of *weltschmerz*."

"No, you're worried about something. Is it grades? Or money? Or your wife and family coming out from New York?"

"No," said Robert. "My grades are good, I drew union scale as an electrician all summer. And my wife and family —"

"Well?"

"They don't know where I am. Isn't that lucky?"

"I never know when you're serious, Robert. Truly, there's no wife and family, is there?"

"I never tell the truth unless I'm quite drunk. And then I talk — paradoxes."

"I've never seen you drunk."

"I'm that object of derision and contempt, the solitary drinker. But then there's nothing more romantic than to sit on the back porch in the moonlight with a bottle of whisky, while the riddles of the universe unravel before your eyes."

Lulu said thoughtfully, "I've never been drunk. Never…What's it like?"

"Oh — the world spins and dances. Sad things are funny and funny things are sad. Music explains things you never knew before."

"It sounds exciting. What about the hangover?"

Robert shook his head. "Not unless you feel guilty. Hangovers are psychosomatic: self-punishment, so to speak."

"Well, well. Isn't that contrary to general belief?"

"All my doctrines are contrary to general belief. I'll never make an engineer. I must have been pretty well oiled when I decided that was the life for me."

"I'd like to get drunk," said Lulu. "Maybe I can come to some decisions too."

"It's illegal," said Robert. "You're only twenty; that's too young. And when I'm drunk I relax my inhibitions. I sing and dance and get in fights —"

"All on the back porch?"

"It's large. I prefer that you remember me as a man with a certain amount of dignity." They had returned to the car. He opened the door, Lulu got in.

"Wait here just a minute," said Robert. He returned presently with a brown paper bag from which he withdrew a bottle. He broke the seal, unscrewed the cap, handed the bottle to Lulu. She took a small gulp, coughed and choked. "Wow! That's strong!"

Robert took a swallow. "Just plain old whisky. Eighty-six proof." He started the car. "I've got ice-cubes and lots of water at home."

"Robert."

"What?"

"Nothing."

They returned across the bridge, drove up dim streets to Robert's apartment. Robert parked, opened the door for Lulu. Slowly she alighted. Already her head felt light from the first nip, and also a second and third she had taken en route. Robert led the way to his garden cottage, flung open the door. "Such as it is, my home."

Lulu came slowly inside, stood uncertainly in the center of the room. The house was clean, but curiously barren of any personal belongings. There were a few books, a yellow dahlia in a white vase, very little else.

Robert turned up the floor furnace, brought glasses, ice, water, and mixed a pair of drinks. He held up his glass. "To your good health. A conventional toast, but a very nice one."

Lulu screwed up her face, gulped down the drink. She squinted around the room. Shapes were tilting and soaring; the dahlia burned with all the ardor of molten gold. She leaned back upon the couch, into the cushions. "Robert."

He seated himself, leaned back beside her. "Well?"

"Have I ever told you the story of my life?"

"No."

"Shall I?"

Robert drank. "If you like." He mixed new drinks.

"First of all," said Lulu, "I'm a murderess. Are you horrified?"

Robert shrugged. "I've discarded all notions of right and wrong."

"It's true. When I was eight years old I shot my uncle. Killed him."

"I never had any uncle to shoot," said Robert regretfully.

"My father was a missionary in Japan…I just vaguely remember living there. We were in a concentration camp and he caught tuberculosis. He knew he was dying and sent me here to live with my aunt and uncle." Lulu blinked. "Everything I remember about Japan is off in a golden haze…He died while I was aboard the ship." Lulu laughed mournfully. "I haven't thought about the Brewers for ages. Uncle Maurice, Aunt Flora. Kendall. Oliver. I wonder what's become of them? Uncle Maurice, of course. He took a gun away from me and began to spank me. I became very upset and pulled the trigger…That was when I was eight." She held up her glass, looked through it. Robert seemed distorted and remote. The lamp glowed with a richer tinge, the dahlia scintillated like a Fourth of July sparkler. Lulu sat up for a moment, then swayed back against Robert. "I'm drunk…But I don't hear the music explaining the mysteries."

"It's not for beginners."

"Right," agreed Lulu. "Why push things? Where was I?"

"You're eight years old, you've just shot Uncle Maurice."

"There isn't much more to tell. Or rather — there's such a lot that I can't tell it. I can't even think about it without getting cramps in my stomach." She was leaning against Robert, he was stroking her hair. "They sent me to the State Home for Girls — reform school. It was an awful place. But I guess there was nowhere else for me to go. Aunt Flora naturally didn't want me." There were tears in her eyes. She sat up, reached for her glass. Empty. She picked up the bottle, hesitated, then gingerly poured a quarter-inch into the glass, added water, swirled the glass, watched the amber ripples swing back and forth. "That's all there is, Robert, until I came to Cal. I've been nowhere, done nothing very exciting. I'm — inexperienced."

Robert sipped his glass ruminatively. Lulu stirred, looked at him. "Now, tell me about yourself."

"There's not much to tell. Middle-class family, high-school, N.Y.U. No brothers or sisters. When my parents died I joined the migration west."

Lulu's eyelids sagged. From a level ever more remote came Robert's voice. She felt warm and, after her tears, emotionally purged. Robert spoke further, in a meditative voice, as if conversing with himself. "And now the glorious future. Have you ever read of the anchorite crab?"

"No," Lulu heard herself say.

"When it's still very small it crawls into a likely chunk of coral and the coral builds around it, and the crab spends the rest of its life immersed in the cell...I've trained myself well; I'll crawl into some salaried niche and spend the rest of my life doing things I really don't give a hang about."

"What do you want to do, Robert?" Lulu's voice was dim and drowsy.

Robert chuckled softly. "What I've got to do."

Lulu murmured something which neither she herself nor Robert understood. Robert eased her down on the couch, removed her shoes, covered her with a blanket.

The light dimmed. From a tremendous distance she heard him settle into a chair; she heard the tinkle of ice, she felt the spinning and reeling of her brain: a spiral nebula, the Great Nebula in Andromeda, spinning, reeling, flashing, glimmering, alone and tremendous in the darkness of space.

CHAPTER IX

SHE AWOKE TO FIND sunlight in the room. She sat up, acutely uneasy. Something she had neglected to do, something urgent, something needful... She looked at the table. Bare. No bottles, no glasses. She rubbed her forehead, ran her fingers through her hair. She listened. Silence.

She got to her feet, looked into the bedroom. No Robert. Mildly puzzled she continued on through the bathroom, washed her face, rinsed her mouth, combed her hair. Then she went into the kitchen, found the coffee-pot, set it on the stove.

A few minutes later Robert came in, with a bag of groceries. He looked a trifle wan, but Lulu noted that he was freshly shaven.

She unpacked the bag: bacon, eggs, grapefruit, fresh doughnuts. "Robert," said Lulu, "you're a poet. Only someone intensely aware and sensitive could make such an effective entrance."

"I knew you'd be hungry," said Robert.

"But I'm a terrible cook."

For several weeks Lulu saw almost nothing of Robert; then they gradually resumed their old relationship. During Christmas vacation Lulu worked at a ski lodge, then the spring semester began: her last before graduation.

On April 18 Lulu reached the age of twenty-one. The day was bright and clear, a Saturday. Robert called for her early in the morning; they drove south to Monterey, and further south still, past Carmel and along the lonesome coast road to Big Sur. They had dinner at Nepenthe, on an open terrace overlooking the ocean. Robert ordered champagne.

"Robert," declared Lulu in astonishment, "have you gone mad? At eight dollars a bottle?"

"Don't forget: I'm a poet. What's money? The banks are full of it."

"You're very strange, Robert…Sometimes I think you're just a trifle mad."

Robert shrugged. "I'd be the last to argue."

Lulu toyed with the champagne goblet. "Robert—last week somebody asked me to marry him."

"And?"

"I said no."

"Was he a good catch? You might have made a mistake."

"Perhaps." Lulu twisted her wine glass. "But I don't care whether I get married or not. Men don't mean much to me. Maybe I'm undersexed. Or maybe…"

"Maybe what?"

"Maybe I love someone else."

"Hmmf…Who?"

"You, naturally."

Robert made a sardonic grimace. "That's a mistake."

Lulu smiled wanly. "Are you going to ask me to marry you?"

"No," said Robert.

"Well, that's definite enough."

"Do you know why? Because I'm not good enough for you. That's one reason."

"Oh, come now, Robert. What an old-fashioned idea. Woman on a pedestal, yet."

"No pedestal. I just happen to be groveling around in the slime. I know myself, you don't. I'm just plain not good enough for you."

"But I think you are, Robert. Isn't that what mainly matters?"

"No." Robert was leaning back in his chair. "I feel guilty every time I come near you. You're beautiful and good and loving and kind—"

"Rats. I'm nothing of the sort. You just don't know me. Robert, are you drunk, or really crazy for sure?"

"I'm not drunk, no! I don't think I'm crazy. I know myself pretty well, and I don't like myself. Whenever I come near you—sometimes I can't help myself—I like myself less than ever."

"I must say, you're an odd case, Robert." Lulu drained her glass with a flourish. "I think I'll get plastered," she said offhand.

"You're not taking me seriously."

"Certainly I am. Suppose I did something terrible — really depraved! Would that make you feel better?"

Robert laughed. "Maybe it would."

"I'll give the matter some thought… I could start by seducing that man over there. Would you wait in the car for me?"

"Yes. No. Confound it, young lady, you're just making fun of me!"

"What in the world have you done that's so awful?"

"You really want to know the truth about me?" Robert licked his lips, watching her intently.

Lulu laughed nervously. "I might as well know the worst."

"Very well, listen. First of all, when I was — oh about fourteen I imagine, I took my father's car out one night. I had a couple drinks and got wild. I was doing about fifty miles an hour and ran into an old colored lady — couldn't see her in the dark — and kept on going. Hit and run. They never caught up with me. But my conscience hurt me. I argued for awhile: what difference did it make? She was dead, why stop and get in trouble? But I'd done wrong and I knew it. Murder. I was bad, and I knew it. Rotten clear through. This was just the start. I decided that since I was bad I might as well be *really* bad. My father worked for the city, at the central maintenance garage. I made a duplicate of his key to the warehouse and early one morning brought out a truck, loaded it with cases of spare parts: piston rings, spark-plugs, condensers, coils. I sold the load for three hundred and fifty dollars. Big-time, still in high school. Little Marcia Hendricks liked me. I said, let's run off and get married. So we did. Lied about our ages, got married by a justice of the peace in upstate New York.

"The marriage lasted three days — the week-end. We had a fight. I said, 'If that's the way you feel, forget the whole thing — tear up the certificate.'

" 'Forget it? How can I forget it after what's happened?'

" 'I'll show you how to forget it.' And I tore up the certificate, with Marcia yelling and crying.

"A year or so later she wanted to get married for real — to somebody else, naturally. She wanted me to get an annulment or a divorce. I told her, don't be bourgeois. Just get married. Which she did. Naturally somebody learned all the ins and outs, and all hell broke loose. Not for me. I'd gone to live with my grandmother in the Bronx. Her husband stormed around, said he was going to shoot me. But when he came to see me, he was all polite and affable: just wanted to talk things over, get our affairs straightened out. What a jerk. She got a divorce, I started N.Y.U.

"So now, the next step. Operation Grandma. The old girl was tight as a wet shoelace. I needed money. Grandma said she couldn't afford a loan. She belonged to the Swedish Lutheran Church, and every Sunday insisted that I go likewise. Grandma was a hard woman and death on alcohol. Early one Sunday morning I took on a snootful and said I was ready for church. Grandma turned blue. The disgrace! I couldn't go to church in that condition! She'd never be able to hold her head up again! I said too bad, church was for all the sons of God drunk or sober, and I planned to go repent my sins this morning. The reason I was drunk was because I was depressed, and I was depressed because I was broke. If only I knew where I could find a hundred dollars every couple weeks I wouldn't need to get drunk. Grandma told me to get out of the house. I said I'd go to church this very morning and blow my brains out in front of the congregation. Grandma wrote me a check: one thousand dollars. 'Take it and get out of my house.' I took it and got out. But I kept my hand in. I went to the church every two or three weeks and crept into the pew beside Grandma. She could never be sure I hadn't come in order to blow my brains out, and her checkbook came out automatically. She died during my sophomore year. All her money went to the church." Robert shook his head, grinned sourly. "That's about all of it. Murder, theft, bigamy, extortion. Did I know I was doing wrong? Certainly."

Lulu was silent a moment. Then she said, "You're quite a case, Robert."

"Quite a case."

"I don't really know what to say. I'm a murderer myself, of course."

"True."

"Still — you're making yourself out much worse than you are."

"I haven't made myself out bad enough."

"Juvenile delinquence, adolescent vapors, sensitivity, guilt psychosis…"

"Not to mention plain ordinary worthlessness."

Lulu laughed forlornly. "I don't know what to say. Except that as far as you and I are concerned — what difference does it make?"

Robert shook his head. "It's hard to explain. Except that you deserve much better of life than me. I've got this guilt-thing under control, more or less; it doesn't force me to keep on proving I'm evil. If I married you — I couldn't live with myself."

Lulu said slowly, "I'm afraid I just don't understand, Robert. Not completely. But you should have told me all this before. And we'd have started therapy."

"I never knew you took any interest in me."

"Now, Robert, that's rather lame. Surely you know better."

The drive back to Berkeley was long and quiet. Robert stopped in front of Lulu's apartment, she leaned over against him. "This foolishness has got to stop, Robert. Unless you don't like me."

"I like you."

"Then the therapy begins right now."

Robert sighed. "If you say." He kissed her.

"Do you feel guilty?"

"Goodnight, Lulu."

"Yes," said Lulu. "It had better be goodnight."

A month later Lulu received a registered letter from Japan. It had been addressed originally to 2413 Belvedere Street, forwarded to the State Home, re-directed to the University of California, and finally to Lulu's present address.

With trembling fingers and pounding heart Lulu tore open the envelope, pulled out the enclosure.

A letter-head caught her eye: Matsuoka and Kuse, Counsellors-at-law. Tokyo.

"Dear Miss Enright," read the letter. "Pursuant to the instructions of your late father who was my valued friend and client, I am now sending you the enclosed communication, which speaks for itself. My best regards. Sincerely, Toshio Matsuoka."

Attached was a second letter, written in black ink in a firm round hand, and it carried Lulu thirteen years into the past, to the cedar-scented old rectory at Onomichi.

My dearest Luellen:

I sit here at my old desk and write into the future; I address the gracious young lady that my little girl must become. It is a peculiar sensation: sad and sweet all together. The idea only just occurred to me as I looked through the screen to see you playing in the sunlight with Kip and Tatters, your kitten and your doll. I will speak to you across the years since I know I shall never be here to speak to you with my earthly voice.

God has been good to me, dearest Lulu: He gave me your mother and He gave me you; but now, in His utter wisdom He sees fit to call me to other shores, and I must obey. Still I cannot but wish my time here were longer. I think of hundreds of matters of which I would advise you, but I feel sure that the teaching of your estimable Aunt Flora — who is, above all, correct — will be of more immediate value than my idle words.

I long to see you — the woman I address. I wonder about many things — and yet as I watch you I know the facts most important. How can you be other than good, loving, kind? Already, as you fondle Kip and nurse your doll there is manifest a wonderful sweetness of character. I would be the last to equate money with happiness, but I trust that the small inheritance I am able to bestow will relieve you — and in time, your own husband and your own dear children — of the annoying little exigencies which, alas, your mother and I have very often known. Twelve thousand dollars I reckon it at current exchange, and I have asked your Aunt Flora to invest it carefully and conservatively. In thirteen years your principal will certainly have grown by three or four thousand dollars.

In the matter of the vase you may or may not remember its history. Your grandfather obtained it by means which I fear were not altogether unassailable, but regarding which I have resolutely refused to trouble myself. (An interesting reflection: ownership to all real property everywhere in the world originally stems from some sort of violent and forcible seizure — without exception. By this I mean the title, no matter how apparently sanctified by legal process, if traced back will ultimately lead to an act of villainy. But this is neither here nor there.)

Back to the vase. It is an authentic treasure, and by now I'm sure you are aware of its value — the exact sum I'm sure I can't guess. Certainly ten thousand? perhaps fifteen, twenty or even more, depending upon circumstances. I suspect that the Imperial House of Japan might prove the highest bidder since (you may or may not recall) the twin to this lovely vase occupies a niche of honor in the Imperial Museum.

Please use the money joyously and I will be happy with you. If you need more money — sell the vase. Spare no sentiment for a useless bauble. Your Aunt Flora I know covets it; if she wants it, do not spare her; insist that she meet the highest outside bid. (Excuse me, Flora dear, if you chance to read this letter. I feel that I must advise Lulu to harden her heart, which, if at all like that of her mother, will be soft indeed.)

Now, my precious little daughter — you now seem to be reading from your nursery rhymes to Tatters — across the years your father speaks to you and wishes you peace and the blessings of a happy and creative life. As sure as the sun shines, rain falls; God exists and is good, so sure am I that I will be watching and rejoicing with you from another realm. Therefore waste no tears for your sentimental old father.

All my love and my fondest hopes,

> *Kenneth Enright*
> *The Rectory, Onomichi,*
> *April 2, 1948*

Lulu sat immobile. She re-read the letter, and in spite of the express admonition, she wept. For a time she lay on her couch looking up out the window, through the fronds of a eucalyptus tree, into the blue sky. If her father actually watched from the regions he described so confidently, his rejoicing must certainly be qualified by a good deal of second-guessing.

Lulu sat up straight on the couch — suddenly furious. Flora Brewer had never mentioned twelve thousand dollars. Where was it? And the vase: she had claimed it as her own, from the moment — even before — Lulu had unpacked her trunk. Lulu clearly recalled that morning thirteen years ago when her Aunt Flora and Uncle Maurice together had opened her trunk and abstracted the vase...Lulu went to the phone and called Robert.

"Hello."

"Robert, can you come over? The strangest thing has happened."

"Strange? In what way?"

"A letter I just received. From my father."

"Your father! I thought he was dead."

"Yes, he's dead. It's a kind of a posthumous communication. It makes me feel all funny."

"I'll come right over."

Robert read the letter, examined the envelope, read the letter once more. "He seems to have been a nice old fellow. Maybe a little wooly."

"That's a description to fit nine out of ten missionaries."

"Your aunt never mentioned twelve thousand dollars?"

"Never."

"And the vase?"

"She told me that my father had given it to her."

"Hmph. Your aunt seems — rather peculiar."

"Peculiar is right." Lulu seized the phone. "I'll find out right now." She dialed.

"Information," said a voice.

"The residence of Mrs. Maurice Brewer, 2413 Belvedere Street, San Francisco."

"The number is GRanada 5-9690."

Lulu dialed once more. Across the bay a telephone whirred.

Flora herself answered. "Hello?"

At the sound of the well-remembered voice, little prickles coursed along Lulu's skin. She controlled her voice. "Aunt Flora? This is Lulu. Lulu Enright."

Flora's voice became remote, excessively polite. "Well, well. This is quite a surprise to hear from you."

"Yes, it's been a long time."

"And how are you?" Flora's voice became almost sugary.

"Very well. And you?"

"I seem to be in good health. The boys will be interested to hear that you called. Are you — ah, are you —"

"I'm graduating from the University in a month or two," said Lulu clearly.

"Indeed! That's very wonderful. I had no idea that, well, under the circumstances —"

Lulu laughed with calculated insincerity. "Oh my yes. And Kendall and Oliver, they've both finished school, of course?"

"They've both done marvelously well. Kendall's in business, making quite a name for himself. He and his wife live only a few blocks away in their new home."

"Kendall is married?"

"Oh yes, he's been married — several years. They have two lovely children."

"And Oliver — did you say he's doing post-graduate work?"

"No." Flora's voice became edgy. "Oliver tried Stanford for a year or two, then Baker and Stevens made him an offer he couldn't turn down. He's marrying shortly himself, a girl from a wealthy old family."

"Speaking of wealth," remarked Lulu, "since I am now twenty-one and no longer a minor, I think that it's about time I took control of the money my father left me — twelve thousand dollars and whatever its increment has been."

There was an instant of silence. Then Flora laughed indulgently. "My dear child! There's no money coming to you."

"And also my vase, which I understand is quite valuable. When can I come after it? I'll come this very minute if it's convenient."

"I'm afraid that you labor under a serious misapprehension. The vase was given to me by your father, as a result of a long outstanding agreement between myself and your mother."

"Frankly, Aunt Flora, I think *you're* mistaken. I have right here in my hand a letter from my father, written just before he died. He tells me the vase is mine, he mentions twelve thousand dollars which he has sent to you in trust for me."

Flora's voice became steely. "I don't care to reopen old sores, Luellen, but perhaps we should have an understanding. First, the vase is mine, that's all there is to it and I won't discuss it further. As to the money, you must remember that you shot and killed my husband. He was on the point of making a considerable sum of money — far more than the twelve thousand dollars from your father. As a result of your act, my sons and myself were not only denied the companionship of their father and my husband, we not only lost the money he was about to earn, but we also suffered a number of extraordinary expenses. Your father sent me the money to invest or use as I saw fit — I have this in writing by the way. I used this money to indemnify myself, Kendall and Oliver, for the loss which you inflicted upon us. It came to four thousand dollars apiece, and I assure you we all regarded the money as the most trifling matter against our great loss. So there the matter rests. You can take no legal action; your father granted me an absolutely free hand. I advise you to forget the whole thing."

"Hmm," said Lulu. "In short, you won't give me either my money or my vase."

"It is not your money and it is not your vase."

"Aunt Flora, you have no legal right and no ethical right to take my property from me. Whatever I did, accidentally, a frightened and hysterical child —"

"You are no longer a frightened hysterical child, Luellen. Accidentally or otherwise you were responsible for the death of my husband Maurice and my subsequent hardships; you must bear the consequences. That is my final word on the subject."

Lulu stared at the telephone, which now clicked and gave off the mindless buzz of an open line.

Robert sat watching, his eyes brooding. "Well?"

"Nothing. The money goes to pay for shooting Uncle Maurice, the vase was never mine to begin with — she says."

Robert grunted. "What a terrible woman."

"Yes," said Lulu colorlessly. "She's hard and egocentric."

"What are you going to do?"

"I'm going to get the money and the vase. Legally, if possible."

The same afternoon Lulu consulted a lawyer, who gave her a pessimistic opinion. "Naturally you can sue — but I doubt if you collect ten cents. Your father very unwisely seems to have given your aunt full discretion as to what use she should put the money. She could claim that she lost it at the horse races and you'd have no recourse. In the matter of the vase, well, she's got it. Possession is not exactly nine points of the law, but it's a good deal."

When Lulu arrived home, she telephoned Robert. "The lawyer doesn't think much of my chances."

"I don't either," said Robert. "What did he advise you to do?"

"Nothing. He said to forget it."

"And are you?"

Lulu snorted. "No, I certainly am not."

After she hung up, she paced aimlessly up and down the room, then went to her desk and wrote a letter to Mr. Kendall Brewer. She found his address in the telephone book, and mailed the letter.

Four days later she received an answer, couched in the most formal of language.

> Dear Miss Enright:
>
> I have discussed the contents of your letter with my mother, and I must say that I adhere absolutely to her position. I cannot see that any useful purpose could be served by the face-to-face interview you suggest. In fact, if I may allow my emotions to intrude into this matter, I should think that you would be ashamed even to bring up the subject of money. My father took you into his home, you callously shot him in the back. Even making allowances for your youth and the 'hysteria' you mention, this is a notably despicable act.
>
> In short, please be specifically advised that there will be neither help nor encouragement forthcoming from me in regard to your claims upon my mother, my brother and myself — in fact, quite the contrary.
>
> Sincerely,
>
> Kendall Brewer

Lulu smiled bitterly. She thought back to the Kendall of thirteen years ago — tall, saturnine, with the pinched adenoidal look of the chronically constipated. Even then Kendall had seemed dignified and poised. "Pompous ass," muttered Lulu, re-reading the letter. A phrase caught her eye; she frowned, read it once again, pondered. Odd. Probably no more than a figure of speech.

She threw the letter down, returned to her books — final examinations were almost upon her. But her mind wandered. She picked up the letter, studied it even more intently. She rose to her feet, walked around the room, then, unable to concentrate, put on her coat, left the apartment and took the bus to San Francisco.

At the offices of the San Francisco *Examiner* she consulted the files of thirteen years before, and as she read a curious feeling came over her: unreality and mild vertigo, expanding to a nameless throat-filling emotion the like of which she had never known: a compound of grief and fury, aching self-pity, the sense of irretrievable loss.

Returning across the bay, she let herself into her apartment, dropped limply on the couch, sat staring into space. Presently she reached for the telephone.

At the third ring Robert answered. "Hello?"

"Hello," said Lulu. "It's me. Can you come over?"

"Sure. What's the trouble?"

" 'Trouble'?"

"Yes. You sound subdued."

"I feel far from subdued."

"Indeed. Well, I'll be over at once."

When he arrived, Lulu was still sitting on the couch. She got up to let him in. He gave her a swift inspection, looked around the room.

"Sit down," said Lulu tonelessly. "I should have made some coffee. I'll put on the pot now."

Robert silently watched while Lulu started the percolator going. She came back, sat on the couch with one leg folded under her. "Look." She gave Robert the letter from Kendall. Robert read it. "Hmm. Your cousin Kendall, loving and affectionate."

"Do you notice anything significant in that letter?"

Robert raised his eyebrows, re-read the letter. "He seems more of a stuffed shirt than I expected."

"He says that I shot Uncle Maurice in the back. I thought at first this was just a figure of speech — an exaggeration... I went to the *Examiner* office, looked up the story in the files. It read something like this: 'Maurice Brewer, socialite and clubman, prominent in financial circles, yesterday was accidentally shot in the back of the neck by his eight-year-old niece Luellen.' The point is, I never shot Uncle Maurice in the neck, front or back." She leaned forward. "I can still see the picture clear as crystal. He came charging at me. I swung up the gun, and it went off. I might have hit his leg or even his stomach. Not his neck. But — I missed him entirely. Somebody else shot him. Somebody else made me suffer for something I didn't do." Tears came to her eyes. "All those terrible years... for nothing!"

Robert made a movement as if to take her hand, restrained himself.

"And now," said Lulu, "they refuse to give me what my father left me. They knew who shot Uncle Maurice; they were happy that the blame fell on me. And now they won't give me my vase, or my money."

Robert nodded slowly, thoughtfully. "Are you going to the police?"

"What good would that do?" asked Lulu.

"Probably none whatever."

"Exactly."

"Then what are you going to do?"

"I don't know. But I'll get what they owe me." Lulu's voice quivered passionately. "One way or another I'll get it. I don't care what I have to do, I don't care if it takes the rest of my life." She laughed without humor. "I've never felt this way before; it's not pleasant. I want to hurt somebody — as much as they've hurt me... I suppose you think I'm wicked."

"No," said Robert. "Of course not. In fact —" once more he made as if to take her hand and once again stopped "— I'll help you. If you want my help."

Lulu shook her head drearily. "You'd better not get mixed up with me, Robert. I don't know what I'm going to do. Or how... You might not like some of the ideas I'm commencing to have."

"Try me. I'm an old hand at iniquity."

"But it may take months, Robert, or years!"

"Two heads are better than one, to coin a phrase."

"But —"

Robert interrupted. "Put it on this basis. If we collect, you can pay me — whatever my services have been worth."

Lulu laughed. "You can have half, Robert. I don't want the money for myself — I merely want to get it away from the Brewers. My money…"

Robert nodded. "I understand. But half is too much. Say, ten percent."

"It's not important," said Lulu. "You realize that I don't care how I get this money. I'll use any means, any weapon I can find — I don't care how discreditable or criminal or immoral."

Robert grinned mirthlessly. "I might think of a few elaborations myself…Basically, I'm rather a rotten sort."

"Please don't blame me, Robert, if you wind up in jail." She went out into the kitchen, brought in coffee. They sat on the couch drinking. Lulu drew a deep shuddering sigh. "I've never hated before. I never knew what the word meant. Kendall. Oliver. Aunt Flora. They have my money, my vase. And one of them killed Uncle Maurice — and let me suffer for it — nine years."

Robert moved uneasily. "Are you absolutely sure?"

"Absolutely. I'd barely lifted the gun when it went off." She closed her eyes. "I can see the whole thing, I can feel it…"

They sat in silence for a few minutes. Then Lulu laughed uncertainly. "All this seems so unreal, so melodramatic. I don't have any idea how to go about this kind of thing."

"The usual method," said Robert, "is to exploit a weakness in the person you intend to despoil. So the first step —"

"Naturally — study the people, learn their weaknesses."

"Exactly."

Lulu shook her head. "And my final examinations just ahead."

Robert rose to his feet. "Let's forget the whole business until after finals."

Lulu assented reluctantly. "If I can."

Chapter X

A WEEK AFTER COMMENCEMENT Lulu met Robert at a coffee house in San Francisco's North Beach. The time was late afternoon, the premises were only sparsely occupied. Lulu arrived first, took a seat in a booth, and ordered tea. A few minutes later Robert's spare outline filled the door. He hesitated, searched around the room, saw Lulu, crossed the floor, stood looking down at her.

"What have you done to yourself? I hardly recognized you."

"Nothing very much, really. Mainly a difference in attitude. I've become feminine, the rest is only detail. A simple — and rather expensive — suit. A touch of make-up. Some this and some that."

"I've always known it," said Robert. "But it's never been so clear and obvious before."

"What?" asked Lulu, far from displeased.

"You're a sorceress. A beautiful blonde sorceress."

Lulu smiled. "Sit down, Robert."

Robert took a seat, pulled a paper from the breast pocket of his coat. "Here's the dossier on Oliver. But one thing bothers me. Shouldn't we give the poor slob a chance to say no before we go to work on him?"

"I did," said Lulu. "Weeks ago. The day after I heard from Kendall, in fact. I telephoned him, asked him bluntly for my money."

"And he said?"

"He hemmed and hawed. He doesn't seem to have Kendall's self-righteousness — but the end result is the same. He says I have no claim on him, that any money he received came from his mother, to take the matter up with her." Lulu daintily sipped her tea. "I told him that I would, indeed I would. He sounded relieved."

Robert gave a dour nod. "So much for Oliver... Here are the pertinent facts. Oliver Brewer, age 26. He works for Baker and Stevens, Commercial Leasing Agents, with the title Assistant Account Manager. Your aunt seems to have selected the job for him, because his colleagues — the two with whom I talked — think he's next to useless as a leasing agent. He keeps a thirty-five foot cabin cruiser at the St. Francis Yacht Club, and has been known to entertain young ladies aboard same. In fact Oliver is quite a playboy. Drives a Sting Ray Corvette, dresses well, enjoys his liquor, and seems generally held in tolerant contempt. His marriage to Consuelo McGavin is to be quite a big thing socially. She's got pots of money in her own right, inherited from her grandmother, and her father is a millionaire. She's no great beauty, if the newspaper pictures are to be trusted, but certainly no reptile. For Oliver it's a good match."

"And the big day —"

"July 30. Followed by a honeymoon in South America."

Lulu nodded. "I can see why Oliver thinks he needs my money. I've figured what he owes me. Four thousand dollars compounded at five percent, thirteen years: seventy-five hundred, plus expenses. Say eighty-five hundred."

"A nice round number."

Lulu regarded him quizzically. "You're grinning like a wolf. I believe you enjoy all this conniving."

"It beats working."

"I hope so," said Lulu thoughtfully. "I bought this extravagant suit and I'm just about penniless."

"In regard to conniving — do you have any ideas?"

"Yes. If Oliver fails to recognize me as his little cousin Lulu, and if he, well, finds me attractive —"

"I think that's a near-certainty."

"Oliver's weaknesses will then be open to exploitation. In this way." She sketched her plan in general terms. "Of course there are technical difficulties." She described them.

Robert reflected. "I think that first of all —" he explained a method by which one of the difficulties Lulu had envisioned could be obviated, and between the two of them a number of ingenious stratagems evolved.

✳

Oliver Brewer, at the age of 26, had become a popular and reasonably personable young-man-about-town, and, until his betrothal to Consuelo McGavin, one of San Francisco's most eligible bachelors. He was tall, loose-jointed, with a short, rather soft torso, long legs and arms; his features were large, in a face narrow except across the cheek-bones. His hair was brown, dry and straight, and already coving back at the temples. Oliver's easy-going, self-indulgent personality lent his expression a degree of charm; he was open-handed with money and knew a great deal about matters to which the members of his set attached importance: restaurants, theaters, key-clubs; yachts, horses, automobiles; wines, liquors and liqueurs; *The New Yorker, Esquire, Playboy*; scandals and beautiful women; artists, their studios; deviates, their salons; bohemians, their pads; newspaper columnists, society scribes, progressive jazz musicians, and night-club comedians.

Oliver long had resisted marriage, for a variety of reasons. He enjoyed his freedom; responsibility irritated him, and then there was the dismal example of his brother Kendall who had become dull and tiresome long before his time. But Consuelo McGavin was something special. First of all she was ridiculously wealthy; second, she was not unattractive, if perhaps somewhat heavy in the hips and legs; third, she would fall heir to a beautiful three-hundred-acre estate in the Montara Mountains back of Hillsborough. Consuelo, or Connie, as she was known to her intimates, was admittedly conservative, even somewhat stuffy. Oliver told himself this could all be changed once they were married. The wedding was only two months off; meanwhile Oliver enjoyed his final days of bachelorhood. He dared not celebrate too conspicuously: eyes and ears were everywhere in a city the size of San Francisco. But occasionally, under precisely the right conditions... For instance, one afternoon after leaving the office he crossed the street to the parking lot, and next to his Corvette he noticed a strikingly pretty blonde girl in an old black convertible. She was sitting disconsolately, obviously unable to start her car.

"Heigh-ho," called Oliver cheerily. "Troubles?"

"Yes indeed," said the girl. "Perhaps you'd like to buy a car?"

"Sure," said Oliver. "I collect antique automobiles; it's one of my hobbies."

"I notice you're not driving one of them."

"This is a young antique. Give it another fifty years." He walked over to the black convertible. "What seems to be the trouble?"

"The starter doesn't want to work."

"Dead battery, probably. No problem there. I'll have Hank slug in a quick charge, and you'll be away in no time."

"Oh, would you?" The girl turned Oliver a look of such melting gratitude that his head swam.

"Yes," said Oliver. "I would and I will. Ah, er — there'd be an hour or two wait. Can I take you somewhere?"

"Oh, no thanks. I'll just sit in the car."

Oliver licked his lips, looked around the parking lot. "There's a cocktail lounge across the street. Suppose we have a drink while you're waiting?"

The girl hesitated, then glancing demurely sidewise, assented. "I feel very bold, drinking with a strange man."

"Not strange, just eccentric. I'm Ollie Brewer, by the way."

"I'm Isabel Johnson."

Oliver instructed Hank the attendant in regard to Miss Johnson's car, and the two of them crossed the street to the cocktail lounge.

They had a martini apiece, then another, and Oliver still another. Isabel Johnson revealed that she had arrived from Idaho only a few days before, planning to stay with her cousin. But her cousin had married and gone to Honolulu, so Isabel was living at the YWCA.

Oliver said he'd heard it was austere though he'd never tried it himself; what about the two of them having dinner somewhere?

Isabel shook her head. No thanks. She hardly knew Mr. Brewer, in the first place, and in the second she was planning to drive to Sacramento as soon as her car would start.

"Why on earth Sacramento?" asked Oliver in wonder.

Isabel cocked her head sidewise. "Because I left my suitcase at the Sacramento bus station, and I don't have any clothes except what I have on. Nothing. No underclothes, no pajamas, nothing."

The idea inflamed Oliver's imagination; he pursed his lips, leered. "What a fix for a beautiful young lady to be in. No underwear, no pajamas." He rose to his feat. "I know how to fix that."

"You do? How?"

"We'll go buy you some new underwear."

"No," said Isabel. "I'm going to Sacramento."

"Very well," said Oliver. "I'll drive you. And we'll have dinner in Sacramento."

Isabel Johnson shrugged, rather provocatively. They left the bar, Oliver brought forth his Corvette and they plunged off toward Sacramento.

The night was warm, the moon was full; they rode with the top down, Isabel's blonde hair streaming in the wind. Oliver looked sidewise at her. "You look like somebody I know, or somebody I've met; I can't think who."

Isabel slid down in the seat. "You look like someone I know too."

"Who?"

"A boy that I simply couldn't stand. He was so pleased with himself, so vain, as to be absolutely insufferable. You're much nicer, and you're just as attractive as he was too."

"Well, well, well!"

In due course they arrived in Sacramento, and drove to the bus depot. Isabel went off to inquire about her luggage while Oliver made a telephone call to San Francisco. Isabel returned to find Oliver looking a trifle glum. Consuelo McGavin had responded rather tartly to his explanations.

"No suitcase," said Isabel brightly. "No clothes, no nothing. They shipped it on to San Francisco. I'm practically denuded."

Oliver's interest revived. "Not in public! Let's find a quietly elegant, or elegantly quiet, place to dine."

"Do you know," said Isabel, "I could use a drink."

"Likewise," said Oliver. "Likewise indeed. What's food, after all?"

They went to a nearby bar, sat at a booth, and Oliver ordered highballs. "Tell me about yourself," said Isabel. "You're not married?"

"Oh no. No indeed."

"Good," sighed Isabel. "I couldn't dream of having an affair with a married man."

Oliver gulped his highball recklessly. Was it to be so wonderfully simple then? What a marvellous situation! What a marvellous girl! He clasped her hand reverently. "I understand exactly," he said. "It's one of those things that just isn't done." His glass was empty; he signaled the bartender.

"Look," said Isabel. "What on earth is that man doing?"

Oliver looked over his shoulder, to see a dark hatchet-faced young man moving along the bar with a sheaf of papers on a clipboard, collecting signatures. "Some sort of petition," said Oliver. "Everywhere you look, somebody agitating."

The young man came to their booth. "A petition to abolish state income tax, in favor of a general sales tax. Care to sign?"

"I'm in favor of that," said Isabel. "I'll sign. Where?"

"Right here, miss."

Isabel signed, passed the petition to Oliver, who glanced at the heading, and signed in the space below Isabel's name. The paper seemed rather rough to his touch.

"Thank you," said the young man. "That's my quota for tonight." He left the bar.

"Curious," said Oliver. "I can't understand how people get so involved in things. Can you?"

"Depends on what the things are," said Isabel mischievously.

"True." He looked owlishly at her glass. "Are you hungry?"

"No. Are you?"

"No. But I know something that's got to be done. Excuse me." He went off to the restroom.

When he returned Isabel had apparently finished her own drink and ordered two more. She raised her glass. "To us."

She drank. Oliver drank. He winced, looked at the drink. "Good heavens. I've had better whisky."

"Oh," cried Isabel softly. "I thought you'd like it. It's a highball made with quinine water."

Oliver made a grand motion. "A great drink, if you've got malaria."

Isabel raised her glass once more. "To us." Looking into the deep shadows of her eyes Oliver felt a qualm of uneasiness. The girl was definitely odd. But so utterly dainty and beautiful. "To us," he cried bravely, and drank.

Shortly after, Isabel said, "We'd better be going."

"Yes," said Oliver dimly. "Let's be going. Time to be — beddy-bye..."

Isabel helped him from the bar. The fresh night air braced him, he staggered across the street with determination, braced himself against the door of the Corvette. "I'll drive," said Isabel. "We'll go somewhere nice and quiet."

Oliver lurched into the car, slumped into the seat. He heard the engine start, felt motion. Lights flickered over his closed eyelids; there was an endless dinning of miles and lights and winds and far-off voices... Oblivion. Time. More oblivion. Light, voices, events. Hands helping him. Softness, ease. Warmth and darkness. He was alone and not alone. He groaned and moaned and slept.

He awoke to a dull headache, in a strange room, under the blankets of a strange bed, stretched beside the warm body of a strange woman. He was nude, he realized. The woman moved restlessly, turned her head. Isabel — was that her name? Isabel Johnson. He looked blearily around the room. Strange. He recollected little, if any, of all this. His eyes focused on a rectangle of stiff parchment, headed in ominous Gothic lettering — MARRIAGE CERTIFICATE.

Oliver drew in his breath with a quick hiss. What was all this? Isabel stirred beside him, opened her eyes. "Ooh!" She held the sheet up under her chin. "Oliver," she said softly, "how's my nice boy this morning?"

"I'm alive," said Oliver dully. "What is that document?"

"Our marriage certificate? Just a marriage certificate."

"You mean we're married?"

"Yes," said Isabel mournfully. "And I so wanted a church wedding. Can we be married again, Oliver, in a church?"

"Good heavens," groaned Oliver. "This is — this is..." Words failed him. "My mind's a blank."

"I don't remember too much," said Isabel cheerfully. "I vaguely remember getting the marriage license, and the justice of the peace, and coming here."

Oliver swung out of bed, wrapped himself in the bedspread, marched across the room, read the certificate: " 'Oliver Brewer — Isabel Johnson'. I don't remember a thing." He looked at her searchingly. "Are you sure we got married?"

"Am I sure?" demanded Isabel. "Certainly I'm sure. Why else would I be here? Do you think I'm a hussy?"

"No, no, of course not…Did we — er, ah — was the marriage consummated?"

"Wow," said Isabel.

"Where the devil are we?"

"Don't you remember? This is Reno!"

Glumly Oliver hauled on his clothes. When he went to the bathroom, Isabel jumped from bed, dressed herself hurriedly.

Oliver returned, sat on the bed with his head in his hands. "There's something very strange…I've never been so drunk before."

"We'd better be starting back," said Isabel. "Right after breakfast."

They ate in a café adjoining the motel. Isabel seemed very cheerful. "In a way it's really lucky for me to have gotten married so soon. My mother wants to come to California with my three little brothers. Now they can stay with us until they find a place of their own. Can't they, Oliver?"

"Um."

After breakfast Isabel insisted on driving. A mile down the road she pulled up at a sign which read:

JUSTICE OF THE PEACE
Marriages Day or Night

"Why are you stopping?" asked Oliver crossly.

"I left my purse here," said Isabel. "Just a minute." She ran inside the ramshackle frame building. Oliver waited.

From the building came Isabel and a thin bright-eyed old man. Gravely he reached into the car, shook hands with Oliver. "Good morning, son, and congratulations. You've got yourself a sweet little girl."

Oliver inspected him unenthusiastically. "You married us?"

"Yes sir. I suppose you was too excited to rightly remember." The old man winked roguishly at Isabel.

"About what time was it?" Oliver inquired, frowning dourly. "I seem to have forgotten."

"Oh — long about midnight or one a.m."

"What a shame to have disturbed you," said Isabel. "But I suppose it's no novelty."

"No, Mrs. Brewer." Oliver winced. "Nineteen years I've been set up here; it's a good living, and honest."

"What of the marriage license?" asked Oliver suddenly.

"All regular and proper. Indeed yes."

"I wonder — do you have it handy? I'd like to look it over."

"Sure thing." The JP went into the house.

Isabel glanced quizzically at Oliver. "You're acting very oddly, Oliver."

Oliver shrugged petulantly. The old man came from the house carrying a folder. "Let's see…Here we are."

Oliver scrutinized the unromantic form. "That's my signature," he admitted grudgingly. He considered the old man once again. "And *I* came in and *I* got married?"

"Sure thing. You was wearing that red-colored coat and that green hat just like you are now, and that brown scarf around your neck."

Oliver shook his head, turned back to the Corvette. "Just a minute," called the Justice of the Peace. He brought forth an old black camera. "Look this way, Mrs. Brewer; you just stand there like that, Mr. Brewer." He clicked the shutter, in spite of Oliver's yelp of protest. "That's for my collection," he told Oliver. "Thousands of pictures I got."

"Let's go," muttered Oliver.

"Goodby," called Isabel, waving her hand.

"Goodby. Drop in next time you're past."

"Ridiculous situation," growled Oliver, as they roared off down the road.

"Yes," said Isabel brightly. "Here we only met each other yesterday, and now look at us, happily married."

"I'm not so happy," growled Oliver. "There's something odd going on. I couldn't have been so drunk as to have forgotten all that. It's never happened before."

Isabel said haughtily. "Exactly what are you suggesting?"

"Nothing…Except —"

"Except what?"

"Oh, nothing."

"You don't seem very happy."

"No. I'm not. This is all too mysterious for me to be happy over."

"I've heard quite enough of your innuendoes," declared Isabel. "Apparently I've made a terrible mistake. Please, let me out of this car. At that service station. I'll take a bus back to Reno."

"No!" growled Oliver. "We've got to decide what we're going to do."

" 'To do'? What is there to do?"

"We could have the marriage annulled."

"After what happened last night? Are you insane? You don't take these things seriously. I was raised very differently."

Oliver slowed the car. "We could get a divorce in six weeks."

Isabel said frigidly, "I happen to be a good Catholic. I made a mistake and now I suppose I'll have to pay for it."

Oliver sighed. "*I* made a mistake and *I'll* have to pay for it. All right then, how much?"

"What are you daring to suggest?"

"I'm asking you, what's your figure?"

"Are you trying to buy me off with money?"

"Yes. Not very much, because I don't have very much."

"You drive an expensive car."

"How much?" demanded Oliver in a brutal voice.

"You're an extremely mercenary man, Oliver."

"How much?"

"It's impossible to set a value on virginity, on religious scruples, on hurt feelings and damaged pride."

Oliver laughed. "I'm sure you can do it if you try. The virginity first. How much?"

Isabel grinned. "Oh — let's say five thousand."

"Ouch. And the religious scruples?"

"Seventeen or eighteen hundred."

"Say seventeen-fifty. That's six thousand, seven hundred and fifty. Now the hurt feelings and the damaged pride?"

"Oh — let's say seven-fifty for the hurt feelings, and five hundred for the damaged pride."

"A total of eight thousand. Is that the lot?"

"Plus expenses for six weeks at Reno. You can save that by getting the divorce yourself."

Oliver halted the car beside the road. "How much?"

"It all depends on the style you want your wife to live in, Oliver. I suppose I could struggle by on a hundred dollars a week with a part-time job."

"Will another thousand cover it?"

"Easily."

Oliver pulled out his wallet, extracted a check, wrote. He handed it to Isabel.

"I've left the name blank. Fill it in any way you like. I don't have that much money in my account, so don't try to cash it before late tomorrow."

Isabel took the check. "Nine thousand dollars doesn't seem to mean much to you."

"It means a great deal. I'll have to sell some securities."

"What about your brother?"

"My brother?"

"Kendall. You mentioned him yesterday."

Oliver laughed. "He's got money till his shoes squeak. But you'd never catch him on a stunt like this. Kendall almost got caught a long long time ago. But he's a changed man today." He laughed again. "I'd almost like to see you work on Kendall. Damned if I wouldn't...Well, do you want to go back to Reno? Or get out here?"

"I'll get out at the next town."

Oliver had a sudden thought. "How do I know you'll go through with the divorce? There can't be any publicity."

"Don't worry," said Isabel Johnson. "Provided this check goes through without bouncing."

"The check is good as gold. Remember, there won't be any more."

"Don't worry, Oliver. I've completely finished with you — financially."

In due course the canceled check was returned to Oliver. He took it up ruefully. Nine thousand dollars — a lesson he'd never forget...*Pay to the order of* — of who? Oliver stared, eyes bulging. Feebly he raised a hand, pinched his lips. *Pay to the order of Luellen Enright.*

He gave a harsh foolish bark of laughter, then choked as the mirth turned bitter in his mouth. "Oh, what a fool!" he cried in humiliation and rage. "What an utter fool!"

CHAPTER XI

ROBERT CAME THROUGH the door of the Black Peacock Café, looked along the line of booths. Lulu signaled to him. On this fine summer morning she looked fresh and clean as new popcorn in sea-blue shorts, a white polo shirt, dark blue sneakers.

Robert crossed the floor with long strides, seated himself. "Am I late?"

"No. I'm early. I've been here an hour and a half."

"Hatching nefarious schemes."

"Worse," said Lulu. "I've been working out a general theory of the subject. Swindling at the present is a fine art. I want to reduce it to a science, with exact formulas to extract money from anyone. More or less painlessly."

"Indeed. How far have you progressed?"

Lulu made an airy gesture. "I think I've established the basic principles."

"You alarm me," said Robert. "In this case, no one is safe."

"Perfectly correct."

"How would you proceed to extract money from me?"

"Poof. You're no challenge. By any legalistic view of what happened in Reno, we're married. Whether you used Oliver's name or not. I could sue you for divorce and bleed you white."

Robert arched his eyebrows in shock. "Indeed, indeed."

"Yes," said Lulu, "you're a sitting duck. As easy as Oliver." She tasted her coffee, made a wry face. "Cold. Cold as my heart. Get us fresh coffee, Robert. We'll charge it to the expense account."

"Then I'll have a doughnut also."

"So will I. Chocolate with nuts on."

Robert crossed the room to the counter, returned with two mugs of coffee and four doughnuts. "Fill me in on this science of hornswogglery that you've worked out."

"It's still vague in spots. And now that I try to explain it, it seems to consist mostly of platitudes."

"That's true of all sociological doctrine."

Lulu sipped her coffee. "My ideas run like this. Money is very valuable. A person will part with it only in exchange for something he considers of equal or greater value."

"Such as more money."

"Such as more money. So, the first step: determine what the victim considers especially valuable, and find some way to provide this commodity. And if this commodity is intangible, negative, or even imaginary, so much the better."

"I agree that the theory is quite vague."

"It's a complex subject, with many special conditions and exceptions. Swindling isn't easy. A poor man has no money, so rich men are preferable targets. What can you sell a rich man? If it's legal he can buy it without your help. So he must be approached through his weaknesses or vices, which, from the standpoint of the swindler with high moral principles, is much more agreeable than taking advantage of his virtues."

"Take the case of Oliver Brewer," said Robert gravely. "His weakness — in which he is not alone — is the seducing of lovely young women. He becomes excited and signs a marriage license application through a hole in what he believes to be a petition. Another of his weaknesses is his lack of tolerance for a mixture of alcohol and chloral hydrate. And when he wakes up he is married!"

Lulu nodded. "The case of Oliver Brewer is hardly a classical example, but in general it exemplifies my theory. What does Oliver Brewer consider more valuable than money? His marriage to Consuelo McGavin. So he pays."

"He pays," said Robert grinning, "and he's still chewing his nails. Did he pay enough? Will they blackmail? Oliver wonders, and approaches his marriage on rubbery legs. Shall he chance it and defy the rascals or play it safe as a bachelor?"

"I refuse to waste sympathy on the Brewers," said Lulu. "Perhaps I *will* blackmail Oliver. He was a nauseating little brute as a child, and really deserves no better."

Robert shook his head. "Anti-climactical."

"Come now," said Lulu. "I'm not learning the swindling trade for the sake of its dramatic values…" She paused, frowned. "Or am I…Well, what's the difference? What have we got on Kendall?"

Robert spread out his notes. "In general it's safe to say that Kendall Brewer is not a popular man."

"Hardly a surprise," murmured Lulu.

"I must say that no one actually admits hating Kendall," said Robert. "But no one claims to like him either." He examined his notes. "Would you like a general summary or the details?"

"What's the summary?"

Robert glanced through his notes once more. "Kendall Brewer is heartless, avaricious, cold as an icicle, a tight-wad, a snob, and a dedicated social-climber. His wife, the former Elizabeth Phipps of Menlo Park, is active in the Junior League. She is reputedly respectable. There are two children, Anthony and Martina, pale gray little ghosts."

"Elizabeth Phipps," Lulu reflected. "I doubt if she's the girl Kendall got in trouble."

"Kendall got a girl in trouble?" Robert laughed incredulously. "This is a new light on Kendall's character."

"It happened long ago — in fact, just about the time Uncle Maurice was killed. I don't remember anything about it — except that Uncle Maurice was insisting that Kendall do the honorable thing, while Kendall and Aunt Flora violently resisted the idea. I don't know what finally happened."

Robert shook his head. "I heard nothing about this. He married Elizabeth about five years ago — a fancy wedding, champagne flowing like water, large write-up in the papers. Since then, less publicity. The Kendall Brewers lead an exemplary life. No drinking except when they entertain, and then only the best. Public conduct formal and restrained. Clothes correct, dignified, conservative. Kendall is old before his time. He sees his mother frequently, his brother — of whom he disapproves — less frequently. His business is — well, it's hard to describe. He calls himself an investment counsellor. Actually, he's a real estate speculator, and apparently very shrewd. He'd knife his grandmother for half a buck. He always has time for the social whirl, and is considered a member of the 'smart young set', as the phrase goes. He lives not far from his mother, in a house recently remodeled in the 'Empire' style — whatever that is. Very fashionable, very elegant, so I'm told." Robert turned a page. "He subscribes to the symphony and the opera, makes the first nights, and seems to have established himself among the elite. But according to a knowledgeable and cynical woman employed as society reporter for the *Chronicle* — and to whom, incidentally, I paid twenty dollars — Kendall is a trifle outside the really in-group. The Brewers have lived in San Francisco only twenty years or so —"

"Twenty-six years."

"— and Kendall is considered just a bit pushy. Also he seems to have a sort of feud going with the Cortin de Barras, who *are* in. De Barra exerts himself to keep Kendall in his place; Kendall plots to circumvent de Barra. Very polite but oh so nasty... Well, that's Kendall and his social activities. Children ride horse, attend private schools. Well-behaved, quiet, incipient little neurotics. Elizabeth the wife skinny, blameless, rather plain, dresses expensively. Kendall drives a Continental, wife has a new Mercedes sedan. Rather a cheerless couple."

Lulu nodded thoughtfully. "The child is father to the man. Kendall as a child was already pompous and egotistical."

"He lives, however, a life of conspicuous rectitude. I forgot to mention that he is a dedicated Episcopalian — church for sure every Sunday. None of the disreputable inclinations which made Oliver such a set-up."

"Yes," mused Lulu. "Oliver was almost too easy. It was hardly sporting. If it didn't happen to be my own money I'd almost be tempted to give it back."

"Kendall I'm sure will give us more of a struggle." Robert smiled grimly. "Your sex appeal will fall on stony ground indeed."

Lulu shuddered. "Oliver was bad enough. Sometimes I wonder what I would have done if..."

"If what?"

"Oh just 'if'." Lulu pushed her mug across the table. "Buy us more coffee. We've got to do concentrated thinking, and need all the stimulation possible."

Robert brought more coffee. "I suppose you plan to apply your 'General Theory of Swindlery'?"

"Certainly. It's so simple — even though it's rather complicated."

Robert brought out a fresh sheet of paper. "Do you have any ideas?"

"One or two. How about you?"

Robert nodded. "One or two."

"Let's start conniving."

Chapter XII

AT NINE O'CLOCK on the morning of Saturday June 20th a Western Union messenger delivered a letter to the home of Kendall Brewer. The colored maid signed a receipt and took the letter into the dining room where Kendall and Elizabeth his wife were finishing breakfast.

Kendall slit the envelope, drew forth an elegantly crisp sheet of paper. The message was inscribed in black ink, in a careful austere hand.

12 Monterey Place
June 19th
Dear Kendall:

The thought has occurred to me often of late that the local social climate leaves much to be desired. On one hand it has become banal to the point of dullness, on the other increasingly undisciplined and accessible to the worst sort of parvenus. Call me a snob if you will, but I believe that careful discrimination in the choice of one's associates is an old-fashioned virtue which badly needs an emphatic re-affirmation.

This all leads up to a project I have been mulling over for several months, i.e.: the formation of a small, rigidly exclusive organization with a constituent nucleus of a dozen or so of San Francisco's most distinguished citizens: conservative intellectuals, social leaders, literati, and so forth. This group would serve as Board of Directors, and exercise control over subsequent membership. As a headquarters I know of a small but beautifully appointed old mansion on Nob Hill, similar to that which houses the Pacific

Union Club, and which can readily be obtained on long-term lease for quite a nominal sum.

I propose that we meet here at my home at precisely 4 p.m. on the afternoon of Saturday June 27, to discuss the project, and if we are in agreement, work out a tentative membership policy, by-laws, social program, etcetera. This will naturally be a very important meeting, as those present — and only those present — will constitute the first Board of Directors. Unless I hear from you to the contrary, I will expect you at the time and place specified above.

Below is a list of those to whom I have sent this letter. As you will note, it has been carefully considered. I think it best that we do not discuss the project publicly, or privately, or even among ourselves, until June 27, as otherwise there may be unwelcome newspaper publicity, and pressure exerted upon us all from individuals who, for one reason or another, have not been included in this organizational group. In any event, I myself will be out of town until Saturday.

Sincerely,

R. Thion Hunter III

Elizabeth, wearing a gray satin dressing gown, watched curiously while Kendall read. "Gracious," she said presently, "what is it that absorbs you so completely?"

Kendall handed her the letter; she read it half-aloud, muttering swiftly through the phrases. "My word!" she said. "Isn't that wonderful! And the people..." She read off the names one by one on the list at the bottom. "Really a very fine group."

"Yes," said Kendall in a colorless voice. "Certainly a good set."

"I wonder how much it will cost." Elizabeth frowned slightly. "Such an affair can't be cheap."

"No," said Kendall. "I wouldn't imagine so. None of the people Hunter lists are cheap people. But — a few thousand dollars more or less — what's the difference?"

"Then you're going to attend," said Elizabeth, although her tone of voice indicated that she had never felt any serious doubt.

"Oh yes," said Kendall. "There's no reason why not. If I don't like the set-up…" He made a careless gesture. "I must say that I've had somewhat similar ideas along these lines. I'm glad to see Hunter's taken the bit between his teeth."

"Hm," said Elizabeth, "I had no idea you and Thion Hunter were such good friends."

Kendall shrugged. "He's a quiet sort. I've seen him here and there, round and about. He never says much but he's got a very keen sense of values."

"Yes," said Elizabeth. "Yes, I suppose so." She glanced down the list once more. "My, my — so many of our friends haven't been approached. The Carrs. The Christopher Bainbridges. The Cortin de Barras —"

"De Barra's a non-entity," said Kendall. "A thruster. I'll see that he's not given an in."

"Very exciting," said Elizabeth. "I'll have to call mother!"

"No," declared Kendall. "Better keep quiet until the thing's really settled. Hunter specifically asks us not to let the cat out of the bag."

Elizabeth nodded dubiously. "I suppose he's right. We wouldn't want the newspapers blowing this thing up."

"No," said Kendall. "By no means. Not yet."

On the following Wednesday Kendall as usual drove downtown to the small but comfortable office he maintained on the fifteenth floor of the Golconda Building. He hung up his hat and coat, notified the answering service of his arrival, settled to his mail. He dealt with each letter in turn, jotting memoranda down the margins, dictating a reply into a recording machine.

About ten-thirty his telephone rang, and Kendall answered: "Office of Brewer Associates, Kendall Brewer speaking."

"Mr. Brewer," came the voice, "this is Jim French, of Westcott Realty — met you a month or so ago."

"Oh yes," said Kendall, though the name evoked no immediate image. "How are you?"

"Fine, thanks. There's a young man in my office who wants to sell us some real estate — country property, ranch-land, something of the sort. It's out of our line, and normally I wouldn't carry the thing further, but there might be something in it, follow me?"

"Not completely," said Kendall.

"Put it this way. If I do you a favor today, maybe you can do me a favor some other time. There's nothing in this for us, but you might be able to work out something for yourself. This young man — Mr. Poole — is up from Gilroy, near the new space laboratories."

"Ah yes."

"I'll send Mr. Poole over; you can talk to him and make your own decisions."

"Very well," said Kendall crisply. "Thank you, Mr. French, and I'll remember you if anything materializes."

"Right."

Half an hour later Mr. William Poole arrived at Kendall's office — a tall dark young man with a relaxed rather stupid expression. He was unshaven and wore highly inappropriate clothes: sun-tan trousers and field-boots with a cheap sports-jacket, a striped shirt and green necktie. Kendall looked briefly up at the ceiling, then indicated the chair beside his desk. Seating himself, he considered his visitor with a cool stare. "Well, Mr. Poole," said Kendall, "what can I do for you?"

Poole seemed unabashed by Kendall's lack of affability. "Mr. Brewer, I take it you're in this business to make money?"

"Naturally."

"Well, I've got a little proposition to put in front of you. There's money in it for you and money for me."

"I'm listening," said Kendall.

Poole hitched his chair forward, Kendall drew back an inch. "I live out of town — might say I'm a country man. Well, my neighbor — let's call him Smith — owned a big tract of hill property, maybe two thousand acres or better. It's not good for much but cattle, or maybe grapes, if you wanted to put in the vines. Anyway Smith died last week and left the property to his daughter. She's been living up north in Redding, taking care of her mother — Smith was divorced. If I figure right, she'll be glad to sell and get it off her hands. Now I know something which is going to make that property a lot more valuable. Get what I'm driving at?"

Kendall nodded. "Certainly. You want me to speculate in this property, and if there should be any profits, divide them with you. If I lose my shirt, you'll apologize."

Poole grinned — unpleasantly, thought Kendall. "That's about it — only there won't be any loss. It's one of these lead-pipe cinches. I'll tip my hand a little bit. This property is right in the way of what's going to be a big real estate development. I think you could get it for seventy-five or a hundred dollars an acre — or maybe just pick up an option to buy at that price. In four months or six months or thereabouts, the price could go up ten times. If you had just an option you'd be sitting nice, even after you gave me my fifty percent."

Kendall laughed. "Fifty percent! Good heavens, man, I don't do business that way."

Poole shrugged. "I can't help it, Mr. Brewer. I got information here worth a lot of money. I want my share of it."

"It seems to me," said Kendall slowly, "that what you are proposing is that we capitalize on the ignorance of Smith's daughter, take advantage of her, for our own profit."

Poole leered offensively. "Don't know about that taking advantage of her — but the profit, sure enough. This world is a hard place — I've been dealt a knock or two, I'll tell you. Well, what do you say?"

"I say that even if everything were as you say, fifty percent is an outrageous cut. You risk nothing —"

"But don't forget, without me — no deal."

"Frankly," said Kendall, "I doubt if any deal exists. Situations like the one you describe are few and far between, and there always seems to be someone else in on the ground floor."

Poole hitched his chair conspiratorially closer. "But these situations do come about, right?"

"Occasionally," said Kendall, moving back once more.

"Well, brother, this is the ground floor. Do you want to get aboard, or shall I talk to somebody else?"

Kendall reflected. "I don't mind looking into the proposition. But your percentage is out of line."

"Even if you make, say, a million bucks? That's what a profit of a thousand dollars an acre would get you, even after splitting with me."

Kendall moved uncomfortably in his chair. "Frankly, Mr. Poole, this sounds — fantastic."

"You never heard of a sharp operator making himself a million bucks?"

"I'm not a sharp operator; I'm a conservative business man."

"Is there any difference?"

Kendall frowned. "Frankly, Mr. Poole —"

Poole rose to his feet, grinning wolfishly. "You're not interested? That's all right by me."

"Thirty percent," said Kendall crisply.

"I tell you what," said Poole. "Let's say if the net profit is under a million bucks, thirty percent. If it's over — fifty percent."

"Make those figures twenty-five and forty percent, and I'll agree at least to look into the matter."

Poole hesitated. "Okay," he said finally. "Write it up."

Kendall raised his eyebrows. "Write what up?"

"I want some kind of paper with this agreement in black and white."

"That's ridiculous, Mr. Poole. How can I make an agreement on a deal which for all practical purposes I know nothing about? I'd have to go into the matter thoroughly. Where is this property?"

Poole shook his head. "You know I can't tell you that, Mr. Brewer."

Kendall laughed scornfully. "How can I investigate the situation? You don't understand me, Mr. Poole, I'm a cautious man. That's how I got where I am. I don't even buy a newspaper without looking at the date first."

Poole considered. "Maybe we'll have to trust each other to a certain extent."

"I should say so."

"Tell you what. You want to look this property over?"

"Naturally."

"Where can I meet you — say, Friday morning?"

"Here."

"Good enough. I'll pick you up at about ten o'clock."

Kendall rubbed his chin. "Tomorrow might be better — or even Sunday, or Monday. I've got some important business Saturday…"

Poole shook his head. "I've got a special reason for saying Friday."

Kendall scrutinized William Poole carefully. Somewhere, somehow a tingle of familiarity about this man. Unsavory sort. Typical member of the great unwashed...But suppose the world were composed only of Kendall Brewers? No. Much better situation as it was: one Kendall Brewer and the pack.

"Very well," said Kendall. "Friday at ten."

William Poole appeared at the specified hour, wearing the same costume as before. Kendall wondered if he had removed it to sleep. They descended to the street, and engaged in a brief dispute. Kendall wanted to drive his own car, Poole objected. "Once these people see that big chop-down hearse, they'll know something's up — right now. We don't want to take any chances on tipping our hand."

Kendall acceded with poor grace, and gingerly seated himself in Poole's old gray sedan.

Poole seemed a sufficiently careful driver, and Kendall gradually relaxed. "Where are we heading for?"

"Down south a ways, below San Jose."

"Gilroy?"

"Yeah." Poole turned Kendall a wondering look. "How did you know?"

"I keep my finger pretty well on what's going on. There's a new government installation going in down there."

"That's right." Poole said no more, and the miles ticked off as they followed the Bayshore Freeway south.

An hour passed, and another, and they came to Gilroy, a town of ten or fifteen thousand, similar in every detail to three dozen other towns of rural California. The countryside was pleasant enough: rolling hills spotted with oaks, the flatlands green with truck farms.

William Poole turned east out of town on a narrow asphalt road, which presently wound up into the hills. Kendall looked skeptically out at the passing landscape. "A man would be a fool to buy in here for even fifty dollars an acre."

"Just wait," Poole declared sagely, "just wait and see."

Kendall moved restlessly in his seat. "I don't think there's anything out here for me."

"Just wait, Mr. Brewer, just wait and see."

The road swept around a bluff; Poole swept an arm down at the valley. "That's where she sits, Mr. Brewer: the great new United States Space Field!"

"Hm," said Kendall. "Very impressive. When does work start?"

"That's what we don't know. But soon enough...And here's the Smith property." Poole laughed — foolishly, thought Kendall. "You see, the name was Smith all the time. Thought I was trying to hold out on you, didn't you?"

"It makes very little difference," said Kendall stiffly. He looked around the landscape. There were definite possibilities here, if, as Poole averred, the valley were to be occupied by a government installation. This could always be verified, naturally.

A dirt road wound back around a bluff to an old farmstead, consisting of a dilapidated house, a barn, a large water tank built of rusting steel, assorted sheds and out-houses. In front of the house was parked a worn green Dodge sedan.

"My word," said William Poole, "it looks like we have visitors."

Even as he spoke, a slender young woman in a blue cotton dress came out of the house. "Why that's May Smith herself," said Poole. "I had no idea she'd be here."

Kendall said drily, "If you had any hope of conducting a quiet reconnaissance, you might as well forget it."

"Well, there's no harm done," said Poole. "She might just be ready to strike a quick deal."

"She might be," said Kendall, "but I'm certainly not."

Poole parked the car. "I'll introduce you."

The young woman approached; Kendall saw that she was quite a pretty girl, with short gently waving blonde hair, good features, and really a remarkably fine figure. Hardly the sort one would expect to find up here in the middle of nowhere.

"Hi there, May," said Poole. "Lemme introduce you to a friend of mine, Mr. Kendall Brewer."

Kendall winced, but acknowledged May Smith's charming little acknowledgment.

"I just got here," she said. "I guess you heard about poor daddy. Isn't it awful? And I've got this big place all to myself. What on earth I'll do with it I don't know. Who wants two thousand acres of foxtail and scrub oak?"

"Well, you never know," said William Poole sagely. "It just might be —"

"Excuse me," said May. "I've got to bring out Pip. He gets so lonesome." She swung into the house and presently came out with a monkey on a leash. It chattered and sprang for Kendall's leg.

Kendall, who detested monkeys, jumped back. May Smith gave the leash a reproving jerk. "Pip, you bad boy, behave yourself. Pip is short for Pipsqueak, Mr. Brewer — don't you think that's cute?"

"Definitely," said Kendall. "Well, Mr. Poole, I think we've seen all we —"

"No, no," said May Smith. "I've just put a pot of tea on the stove; you must come in!"

"Sure," said Poole. "Why not?"

"Here, William, take Pip and put him someplace out of mischief. I can see Mr. Brewer doesn't care for him. Now you come inside, Mr. Brewer, and we'll let William deal with that pesky monkey."

Kendall reluctantly allowed himself to be ushered into the house, while Poole marched away with the furious and hopping Pip.

May Smith had boiled a pot of water on a gasoline camp stove. The interior of the house was dilapidated and evidently had been unoccupied for years.

"I thought your father lived here," said Kendall.

"No, not since his second wife left him," said May Smith cheerfully. "And do you blame her, way out here in the sticks? Sugar, Mr. Brewer?"

"No, thanks." He rubbed his chin. "How many acres in the property?"

"Two thousand and one hundred. All up and down. And is it hot in the summer!"

"I take it you don't plan to live here yourself."

"Me? Not on your life!"

"It's just possible I could dispose of the property for you. I won't say definitely, of course — but there are eccentric people in the world." Kendall laughed. "They'll buy anything if the price is right."

May Smith laughed. "Oh, I'll sell — and no argument about price either. The only thing. I promised William first chance on the place." She went to the window. "What in the world can William be doing with Pip?"

William Poole came in the house to answer for himself. "You and your blasted ape," he told May aggrievedly.

"Whatever is the trouble?"

"I thought to put the little monster in my car, but he grabbed the keys and ran."

"Oh, the bad monkey!"

"That's not the worst of it. He climbed the ladder to the water tank, threw them in and that's where they sit."

May laughed nervously. "There's no water, luckily."

"It's a nuisance! You know me and heights."

"Yes. Pip is very bad. But Mr. Brewer won't mind fetching the keys."

Kendall rolled up his eyes in annoyance. He set the cup firmly down in the saucer. "I think we'd better be leaving."

"Suits me," said Poole. "You'll have to climb for the keys. I can't stand heights."

"Very well," muttered Kendall. "Let's get the blasted keys and go."

They went out to the water tank. William pointed out the wooden ladder, by which the top flange could be reached, and the rope ladder to be dropped over into the tank itself. Kendall shook his head grimly, started up the ladder, which seemed extremely rickety. He gained the top flange of the tank, fifteen feet above the ground, looked down into the tank, which, as May Smith had mentioned, was quite dry. He dropped the rope ladder down, gingerly descended. Now — where were the keys? He walked around the circumference, and the metal echoed plangently to his foot-steps. There — the keys. He picked them up, returned to the ladder. He rested his weight on the first rung, and something seemed to give. He looked up doubtfully, tested the ladder again. Was it safe? He put his weight on the bottom rung — and the ladder broke, fell back in his face. Kendall barked an expletive of annoyance and alarm. Then he shouted. "Poole. Hey, Poole!"

There was no immediate response. Kendall stood in the center of the metal cylinder, glaring up at the disk of blue sky fifteen feet above. "Poole!"

Silence.

Kendall tried again, bellowing with all his might, and this time he elicited response. Poole's voice came deep and almost sepulchral through an outlet pipe at the bottom of the tank.

"Was you calling, Mr. Brewer?"

"Damn right I'm calling. The ladder broke!"

"Listen, Mr. Brewer — I was just talking to May Smith. I think she's ready to sell, or at least give up an option to the place."

"I don't know that I'm interested. Certainly not while I'm in this tank. Throw me over another ladder."

A moment of silence. "Mr. Brewer, I don't want to seem disobliging, but I just can't bring myself to climb a ladder. I'm scared of heights."

"Well, get the young lady out here. She's perfectly able-bodied."

"I'll ask her, Mr. Brewer."

A moment passed, then Poole's voice came hollowly once more through the pipe. "Mr. Brewer, she's expecting a baby, and she says she doesn't dare climb a ladder."

"Baby! I had no idea she was married. Is she?"

"Oh yes, she's married. Her husband runs a pet shop. That's where she got the monkey."

"God-damn the monkey. Throw me over a rope, I'll pull myself out."

"Mr. Brewer, I just now asked May how much she'd take for an option. She was just a little unreasonable, but since we're going to pick it up anyway, what's the difference. She says nine thousand dollars."

Kendall stood stock-still. "Nine thousand dollars? For what?"

"She gives you three months' option on her rights to the property. I think you better snatch at the chance. It's cheap, when you come to think of it."

Kendall thought carefully for several moments. Then he said, "Throw me over a rope. I can't talk about it here in the tank."

Poole's voice came hollow and regretful. "Mr. Brewer, I'm afraid of you. That's being frank, but there it is. Now you know everything I know. What's to stop you from closing the deal over my head? I'd like to see you pick up the option here and now — while I kinda know where you are. That's the business-like way to handle the matter."

" 'Business-like'?" Kendall's voice was hoarse. "You want me to take an option while I'm stuck here in this tank? You're crazy. Now get me out or I'll have you arrested."

"That's hardly friendly, Mr. Brewer," said Poole reproachfully. "And really, when you think of it, you can't arrest me for something I haven't done, now can you?"

"Get me out of here!" spat Kendall grimly. "I've got important business waiting for me back in town."

"There's nothing I can do, Mr. Brewer. I don't dare climb the ladder, I don't have no rope nor anything else. Looks like you're stuck for a spell, until I can make a trip into town. Or until things straighten out."

"Just what do you mean?"

"Well — like I say, I can't really trust you not to do business over my head. But there's another man in San Francisco who sounded interested. I think I can deal with him, and if I can, then there's no reason why you shouldn't go free as a bird. In a way it was a lucky thing for me you locked yourself into the tank."

"In other words," said Kendall bitterly, "if I don't take the option, you keep me here. Do you realize that's kidnapping? A serious offense?"

"No such thing, Mr. Brewer. I didn't put you there. You climbed in of your own free will."

"I'll give you one more chance," stated Kendall. "Let me out of here and I'll forget the whole matter —"

"Just a minute, Mr. Brewer," said Poole. "I see May Smith. I want to talk to her."

Five minutes passed. Kendall made futile attempts to cast the ladder over the edge of the tank in the hope it might catch and support his weight.

Poole spoke through the pipe. "Mr. Brewer, she's given me the option — wrote it out in both our names. Just write me a check for nine thousand dollars, push it through the pipe and I'll pass through the option."

Kendall said shortly, "I'll see you in hell first."

Poole made no reply.

Twenty minutes passed. Half an hour. Kendall suddenly raised his voice. "Hey, Poole."

"Yes, Mr. Brewer."

"Let me out of here. I think we can talk business."

"I don't dare climb that ladder, Mr. Brewer. Really it scares me."

"You can't keep me here forever," said Kendall.

"I'm not keeping you anywhere, Mr. Brewer. You accidently got stuck in a tank, and I'm not able to help you. Tomorrow I'll see this other man and if everything goes well, I'll sure do something to help you out."

"I can't wait till tomorrow," shouted Kendall. "I've got a very important meeting to attend."

"I'm sorry, Mr. Brewer. Business is business. Now that you know about the property I just couldn't trust you not to go over my head."

"Nine thousand dollars, eh?" said Kendall. "Very well. I'll write you a check."

"Make it out to cash, Mr. Brewer."

Kendall wrote the check, pushed it through the pipe. "Now let me out of here."

"Not as easy as that, Mr. Brewer. I'll have to take this check in and cash it. As soon as I have the cash I'll rush right back. What I mean is, if you didn't write this check just right, or left off a secret mark, or signed it the wrong way, it's just wasting time."

Kendall was silent.

"Well, Mr. Brewer? Can I cash the check?"

"No."

"I didn't think so…Well, the sooner you write me a good check, the sooner we'll be finished. And don't forget, the banks close at six tonight. If I can't cash it tonight you'll be here till Monday."

"Very well," said Kendall in a trembling voice. Another check came through the pipe. "You can cash this."

"Excellent," said Poole. He pushed a paper back through. "And here's the option. May wasn't quite sure how to describe the land, so she's giving you dibs on any and all property she may own in the entire county. Fair enough, eh?"

"Fair enough," said Kendall dully. "Go cash the check. The sooner you go, the sooner you'll be back." A sudden bitter thought came to him. "The keys — do you need them?"

"Why yes, you can toss them over, Mr. Brewer. Although I guess that somewhere I've got an extra set."

✳

Kendall arrived home at eight, haggard, dirty, very much out of sorts. A letter which shortly arrived by messenger exacerbated his mood.

Dear Kendall: (read the letter)

After careful consideration I have decided to carry the idea I broached last week no further. Not that I decry snobbery; I too am a snob. But, snobbery is a state to be deserved, earned, attained, by achievements which legitimately raise one above the ruck. Then it is a normal, satisfactory and praiseworthy state of affairs, the obverse side to Fame. After contemplating my list of 'directors' I perceived that none possessed the slightest justification to the proud state of snobbery. I suggest, Kendall, that you join the Lions Club.

There was no signature. Kendall crumpled the letter in a rage that prickled his skin like a clammy cold sweat.

The telephone rang. Kendall answered, and a soft feminine voice asked for Kendall Brewer.

"Speaking," barked Kendall.

"This is Lulu, Kendall. Thank you for everything."

"I see," said Kendall slowly. "You're very clever."

"Thank you, Kendall. Do you know that I never killed your father?"

"But you did."

"No. I did not. I want to find out who did. I owe him — or her — a little extra."

Kendall made a gruff sound in his throat. "You're talking crazy."

"Where were you when your father was killed, Kendall? Do you remember?"

"In the house."

"Were you alone?"

"Yes."

"So you don't know what anyone else was doing?"

"No."

"Goodby, Kendall, for now. Believe me, you got off very easily. Much easier than I did."

The line went dead. Kendall, sucked dry of life, sank into an armchair, sat staring into the fireplace, which was dead and dark.

His wife came into the room. "Kendall? You're very quiet."

"Yes," said Kendall. "Get me a glass of sherry. A large glass."

Elizabeth wonderingly obeyed.

CHAPTER XIII

"My aunt has many disagreeable qualities," said Lulu. "It's true that I haven't seen her for many years, but she is impossible to forget."

"She must be a remarkable woman," said Robert drily.

Lulu agreed. She slowed the car, pulled over to the side of the Great Highway, parked. The time was four-thirty, on a warm afternoon. The air was still, the Pacific rolled blue-gray and quiet far out to the west, with blinding slivers and shivers of sunlight leaping and playing everywhere.

Lulu leaned back, stretched luxuriously. "Robert, we're rich. Do you realize this? Filthy rich."

"So far we've escaped jail."

"Naturally. We've done nothing illegal."

"Ha, ha. Wait till the Income Tax people visit you!"

"Rats. The tax has been paid on this money over the years, by Kendall and Oliver. It's one of the small services they were happy to provide."

"Something terrible is sure to happen."

"Robert," said Lulu, "you're in a pessimistic mood."

"I'm beginning to feel the strain of riding a run of luck."

"Luck my eye. We've got the General Theory of Swindlery, High-grading and Informal Confiscation working for us."

Robert made a dubious sound. Lulu leaned back in the seat, gazed lazily across the ocean. "Look at all the water, Robert. Miles and miles... And look at those little white clouds just over the horizon. If we were under them, they'd fill a quarter of the sky."

"Very impressive."

"With all this money," Lulu went on, "we can travel. Anywhere. Tasmania. Zanzibar. Copenhagen."

"Maybe we'd better abscond while we're still out of jail."

Lulu shook her head with an introspective half-smile. "Kendall and Oliver were just practice. Aunt Flora is the main event."

"She'll be a hard nut to crack. Kendall and Oliver undoubtedly have alerted her."

"I don't mind. If I don't succeed the first time I'll try again, and work at her till I get my money. I'll make her so insecure she'll hate to leave the house."

"Vindictive little cuss, aren't you."

"Yes."

After a moment Robert said, "I don't blame you."

"I don't blame myself."

"And how do you propose to proceed? By the General Theory again?"

"Unnecessary. I know exactly how to deal with Aunt Flora."

"Indeed."

"Yes, indeed. Once again we make use of your talents, you did so well as the avaricious lout."

"Simplicity itself, since this, more or less, is my basic nature. A slouch, a leer, a relaxation of the jaw, a twitch of the nose."

"First," said Lulu, "there's the usual preliminary work to be done."

At noon on Wednesday, July 1st, Lulu and Robert parked across from 2413 Belvedere Street in an ancient black panel truck, on the sides of which were painted:

OSCAR ANDERSON
Plumbing Contractor

and disposed themselves where they could watch the entrance.

"So that's Aunt Flora's house," said Robert.

Lulu nodded somberly. "Nothing's been changed in thirteen years, not so much as a geranium. Everything looks much smaller." Lulu looked back across the years, and saw a small sober-faced girl with blonde hair in pigtails arriving in Uncle Maurice's big black sedan. The house had seemed enormous, towering up in front of her like a cliff, grand beyond all her previous experience. "How long ago," said Lulu half under her breath, "and yet — it wasn't really so long."

"Look," said Robert. "Who is that? Aunt Flora?"

"No," said Lulu. "That's the house-boy. Are you blind?"

"Just wanted to make sure."

Up along the walk to the side of the house came a middle-aged Filipino, wearing a natty brown suit and a black hat. "Good heavens," muttered Lulu.

"What's the trouble?"

"That's Giorgio!" said Lulu in amazement. "He's been here all these years!"

"What's so amazing about that?"

"You can't imagine the problems Aunt Flora used to have with her help. None of them would put up with her more than a week."

Giorgio set off smartly down the sidewalk.

"His afternoon off," said Lulu. "Make a note."

An hour passed, two hours. A taxi pulled up in front of the Brewer house; the driver alighted and went up the walk, into the vestibule. He rang the bell and waited. Two minutes passed. In the shadowed vestibule the driver fidgeted. He rang the bell once more, waited another two minutes, then marched fretfully back to his cab.

A window of the upper bedroom flung up. "Hoo-hoo!" came the musical call. "Just a moment. I'll be down shortly."

The driver stared up somberly, entered his cab, thrust down his flag.

"Dear Aunt Flora," giggled Lulu. "Still in form."

Ten minutes later Flora appeared from the house, erect and regal. She closed the door, tested the lock, came down the walk.

Lulu's blood pulsed in her throat. A peculiar numb feeling came over the skin of her hands and face. "That's Aunt Flora," she whispered.

Flora entered the cab, gave crisp and decisive instructions. The cab moved off.

Lulu heaved a sigh. "Now I know how a cave-woman felt when a saber-tooth tiger walked in front of the cave... I'm still terrified of her."

"She's an impressive woman," said Robert. "Rather handsome, in a purse-mouthed sort of way."

"Aunt Flora always managed to cut a good figure. She's a little heavier and not quite as brisk. Otherwise — the same Aunt Flora. Even her clothes look the same. Expensive, just a bit old-fashioned."

Robert looked up and down the street. "Now what? The house is presumably empty."

Lulu nodded. "Go ahead. I think you'll be less conspicuous by yourself."

Robert got out of the truck. He was wearing a pair of blue and white striped coveralls and a black cloth cap. From the rear of the truck he took a tool-bag, crossed the street and turned into the walk-way leading to the rear of the Brewer house. Lulu, sitting stock-still, watched nervously. Ten minutes passed. The front door eased open. Lulu jumped from the truck, crossed the street, ran up the walk, along the vestibule hung with pots of maiden-hair fern, and into the house.

Robert closed the door behind her. They stood in the dim entry hall, and the years were as nothing. Lulu was once again eight years old, coming into the strange big house, rich with its odors of camphor-wood, incense and — still? — the hint of rose sachet.

Robert said, "The service door was unlocked. It was so easy I thought we'd better seize the opportunity, which might not occur again."

"Right," said Lulu. "Did you check the house?"

"Nobody's home."

Lulu still stood with her back pressed against the front door. "This place scares me. I'm absolutely demoralized." She laughed. "But that's not getting our swindling done." She crossed the room. "There it is, beside the Buddha. It probably hasn't been moved a quarter inch."

From the tool bag Robert brought a camera, which he proceeded to focus.

"Shall I move it?" asked Lulu.

"It's okay where it is…Here's the scale." He gave Lulu a folding rule, which Lulu opened and held vertically beside the vase.

Eight times a flash-gun filled the room with white light. "That should do it," said Robert.

"Let's go," said Lulu. "This place gives me the willies."

"Just a minute," said Robert. "We'll never have the luck to find that service door open again. I wonder if there's an inconspicuous window we could leave unlatched, to facilitate our next move."

Lulu hesitated. "Suppose someone finds it…But you're probably right. In the basement there should be such a window."

She led the way through the dining room, walking on tip-toe past the great walnut table. She stopped and pointed. "That's where I used to sit — right there. Kendall — Oliver — Uncle Maurice — Aunt Flora. Jolly little group."

She went to the rear window, looked down into the back yard. "Right there — under the maple-tree — that's where Uncle Maurice was killed. And that's the house where my friend Chickie used to live. Professor Chickweed, and his cat Purr. Poor miserable little Chickie." She stared down at the well-remembered scene. "When I think how Kendall and Oliver used to act..." She shook her head. "I guess I'm too sentimental for my own good."

"We'll both feel sentimental if your Aunt Flora catches us admiring her view," said Robert.

They descended the kitchen stairs into the basement. Robert went to a dusty little window overlooking the walk-way, peered out. "This should do very well." He snapped the latch, tested the window. It raised without difficulty, the sash-cord rattling softly over the pulleys. He closed the window; they returned to the first floor and departed.

While Edgar Varese studied the color slides through a viewer, Lulu looked around the studio. An interesting place, full of fascinating machines and materials. Along the wall by the windows were a pair of potter's wheels, a lathe, a workbench supporting a small ball-mill for the grinding of glazes, a pair of electric test-kilns, bins containing clay and minerals. On the opposite wall shelves supported kiln furniture, bottles of glaze and under-glaze, stains, modeling tools, packages of raw chemicals.

Varese, the ceramist, was a small dark man, sinewy of arm and shoulder. He asked, "You want two of these?"

"Correct," said Lulu. "Identical to this one in the photographs."

Varese cocked his head dubiously. "Let's say a close approximation."

"Very well. A close approximation. The size you can take off of the rule in the photograph."

Varese studied the photograph. "It's Chinese, apparently. In fact, obviously Chinese, in the context of that Buddha next to it. What is that glaze? Do you know?"

"I've no idea," said Lulu. "As you can see, it's a pale lavender, more blue than pink, and it seems smooth, glossy, very deep, very transparent."

"Certainly not a celadon. I've never heard of lavender celadon. Green of course. Even gray."

"Celadon, I think that's what it is. A unique version of this glaze, so I'm told."

"That I can well believe. Well, I can't duplicate it exactly, not in a hurry, that is to say. Give me a year and ten thousand dollars, I'll come close."

"I had planned only a very small fraction of both," said Lulu.

Varese nodded. "So I imagined. Well, I can come close. The body is simple enough. We've come a long way since those early craftsmen. They knew nothing but trial and error. That's the fascination of this business. You never know how a batch has turned out till you open the door of the kiln."

"Back to that year and the ten thousand dollars — what fraction of each will you require?"

"Oh — about a week and two hundred dollars. How does that sound?"

"Within reason. Here's another photograph of the vase: the bottom. Notice this mark? I'd like the identical mark on the bottom of each vase, and nothing else. Not your personal signature, for instance."

Varese turned a careful scrutiny upon Lulu, then shrugged. "Whatever you like. If you can sell them as genuine, let me know. I'll go in the business."

"Mr. Varese! Do you take me for a swindler?"

"Such creatures are known. But — 'Judge not lest ye be judged.' Who among us is without sin? Let him cast the first stone. So long as his house isn't constructed of glass."

"Mr. Varese, you are a profound thinker as well as a master potter."

"Exactly the same thing, my dear young lady."

The printer regarded Lulu with a dull eye, rubbed his chin with a stained finger. "Sure, I can print up a dozen of these, but it won't come cheap. You could have a thousand for just a few bucks more."

"I need only a dozen," Lulu told him, "but I'd like them as soon as possible."

The printer studied the layout. "Picture of the guy here, the vase here, the text just as is. Say tomorrow at 4 p.m."

Three days later Flora Brewer found in her mail a long handsome envelope containing an impressively printed announcement:

The Institute for Oriental Studies announces a series of illustrated lectures by the distinguished Orientologist, Dr. Malcolm Cumberland, recently arrived in San Francisco after intensive study in Japan.

Dr. Cumberland's topic will be:

The Evolution of Chinese Porcelain

ADMISSION BY SUBSCRIPTION ONLY.

Near the top of the announcement a photograph depicted a dark young man with keen ascetic features, a sad sensitive mouth, brooding eyes below saturnine eyebrows. The photograph was labeled 'Dr. Malcolm Cumberland'. Near the bottom was another photograph, labeled 'Sung Vase'.

"Well, well," thought Flora, "I must see about attending these lectures. He looks rather young for an authority, but these days youth will be served... Strange, the Institute makes no mention of time or place. But I'll probably receive further notification..."

On Tuesday afternoon Lulu returned to the studio of Edgar Varese, master potter and philosopher. On a shelf in the anteroom she found an identical pair of graceful vases, glazed a transparent pale gray-violet.

Varese appeared as Lulu was examining them. "Well, do they suit you? Will they suffice?"

"Yes," said Lulu. "You have done very well, Mr. Varese. The glaze is — I *think* — just a little brighter than the original, but the difference is trifling." She looked at the bottoms. "The marks —"

"Both the same, according to your instructions."

"Excellent." Lulu wrote a check, took the vases, one in either hand, and departed.

The following day was Wednesday, and the old black panel truck once more parked across the street from 2413 Belvedere Street.

Shortly after one o'clock Giorgio came up the side passage, natty in gray sharkskin of exaggerated styling and a soft black fedora.

An hour passed; two hours. Lulu became restive. "Is she planning to stay home all day?"

"Some people do," said Robert.

"Perhaps she went out this morning and hasn't returned yet."

Robert shook his head. "I think not."

Lulu looked at him in irritation. "How can you be so sure?"

"Logic. If she were gone would the house-boy wait till after lunch before taking off? Not much. He'd be off like a shot as soon as the door closed behind her."

"Not necessarily," said Lulu. "Aunt Flora is a great one for arranging duties and chores. She'd leave him enough work to keep him busy all day."

"We could telephone and see if she answered," Robert suggested. He looked up and down the street. "I don't suppose there's a service station for blocks."

"Look," said Lulu. "Here comes a taxi. She's leaving."

Five minutes later Flora Brewer had ensconced herself in the cab and had been borne away.

"The house is empty," said Lulu. "Robert — to work!"

"I hope the window is still open," said Robert. "Otherwise — it's breaking and entering." He took his tool-bag, got out of the truck, sauntered across the street, disappeared down the passageway.

Lulu, listening intently, heard the faint rattle of a window being raised.

A moment later the front door eased open. Lulu left the truck carrying a card-board box. She entered the house, paused in the dark-paneled entry to let her eyes adjust to the gloom. The grandfather clock clicked and chimed; the two jerked nervously. From the box Lulu took a vase, carried it across the room to the big gilt Buddha.

"For heaven's sake, don't mix them up," said Robert.

Lulu laughed. "What a joke. Actually, they're hard to tell apart." She made the substitution, stood back. "Who would know the difference?"

"Let's not admire our handiwork," said Robert. "Time is passing; your aunt may have merely gone out to mail a letter."

"True," said Lulu. She tucked the original vase in the box, carried it tenderly from the house.

That very evening Flora Brewer received a telephone call. "Mrs. Brewer?"

"Speaking."

"This is Marian Rutledge, secretary to The Institute of Oriental Studies."

"Oh? I'm not sure —"

"We've met several times, I believe."

"Oh yes," said Flora distantly.

"You've probably been notified that Dr. Cumberland is lecturing."

"I received the announcement. But —"

"The museum is showing some of Dr. Cumberland's private collection. I hope you'll forgive me, Mrs. Brewer, but I mentioned your marvellous Sung vase to Dr. Cumberland. He was intensely interested, and I think you'll be hearing from him personally."

"Well, indeed," said Flora, but in a voice of no great hostility. "I suppose there's no harm in that. I shall be pleased to talk to Dr. Cumberland, although my own collection is not at all extensive."

"That's very good of you, Mrs. Brewer. I *do* have a wagging tongue and I was afraid you'd be offended."

"Not at all, not at all," said Flora graciously.

"Very well, Mrs. Brewer, and we'll look forward to seeing you at the lecture."

The phone went dead before Flora was able to inquire when and where the lectures were to be held. And which Institute was it? The Asia Institute? Oriental Art? Something of the sort.

Half an hour later the telephone rang once more. A masculine voice spoke. "Mrs. Brewer? This is Dr. Malcolm Cumberland speaking."

"Oh yes, Dr. Cumberland. I understand you're lecturing at the Institute."

"Yes, lecturing and conducting a seminar at the University, before I leave for the East. Mrs. Brewer, I heard a curious story today, and I must say I'm tremendously anxious to see your Sung vase. If it's the same vase I think it is — well, I'll have something interesting to show you."

"Dr. Cumberland, you sound so mysterious."

"Perhaps I could call tomorrow, about eleven?"

"I'd be delighted. Perhaps you'd stay for luncheon."

"I'm afraid that's impossible, thank you nonetheless. But I'll look forward to seeing you at eleven o'clock."

"Very well, Dr. Cumberland."

At the time appointed a young man, somber of expression, conservative of dress, parked a handsome black sedan in front of 2413 Belvedere Street. He alighted, walked to the front door and pressed the bell-button.

He was admitted by the house-boy and conveyed to the second-floor sitting-room, where Flora Brewer awaited him.

"Dr. Cumberland? You're rather younger than I expected."

Dr. Cumberland bowed gravely. "I'm afraid I find my age a handicap in certain respects. I have devoted twelve years to the study of Chinese and Japanese ceramics, and occasionally I find it difficult to convince older persons of my qualifications."

Flora gave him a cool smile. "You need fear nothing of that sort here. I understand you've just returned from Japan?"

"Yes, I've been back in the States only a week or two. And already I'm homesick."

"I myself was born in Shanghai," said Flora, "and I'm well acquainted with the spiritual doctrines of the Orient. Perhaps I can offer you some tea, Doctor? I have a fine smoky Lapsang Souchong which I don't ordinarily serve my guests, but which I'm sure you'd enjoy."

"I'd be delighted, Mrs. Brewer, but first — may I examine your Sung? Curiosity is devouring me."

"Certainly. We must return downstairs."

Flora led the way back down the entry hall, pressed a switch which surrounded the gilt Buddha in a rectangle of diffused golden light.

On the table before it rested the gray-violet vase. "Ah!" cried Dr.

Cumberland in high excitement. He advanced swiftly across the room, picked up the vase, examined the bottom. "My dear Mrs. Brewer, what a surprise this is! What a wonderful discovery!"

Flora gave a cool ladylike little laugh. "I'm aware the vase is very valuable."

"And I'm sure it has an exciting history. I'll be glad to drink a cup of tea now."

"Of course." Flora raised her voice. "Giorgio! Tea please!"

They returned upstairs. "I'll tell you my little story first," said Dr. Cumberland. "It's a strange story, and it puts me in a rather equivocal position — but I won't apologize. We're both collectors, after all. Well, to continue. Naturally I've visited the Imperial Museum in Kyoto, where I struck up quite a friendship with one of the custodians. To make a long story short, I was on the point of returning home — in fact, I was already aboard my ship — when this custodian visited me, carrying a parcel. He was frantic, desperate. His daughter was dying of cancer, he needed money desperately. He had decided to sell one of his private treasures, so he informed me. He opened his bundle, and lo and behold, a Sung vase in the almost unique violet celadon. I asked him his price, it was ridiculously low. I paid him. As he was going out the door, he turned back, 'Dr. Cumberland,' he said, 'you are entitled to the full story of that vase. It is one of a pair. Many years ago, the mate was stolen by Chinese bandits and sold. Alone this vase is a prize; the matched pair would be an inestimable treasure.'

" 'Indeed,' I said. 'Who owns the other vase?'

" 'That no one knows. It was sold to an English family and taken to America, and passed from sight.'

"Naturally I suspect that the man had stolen this vase from the Imperial Museum. But I have no proof. I prefer to believe it was his to do with as he chose. So, Mrs. Brewer, you can imagine my shock when Mrs. Rutledge saw my vase and remarked that it resembled one in your possession."

"How absolutely fascinating," said Flora, her eyes glittering. "And where is your vase?"

"I brought it with me, and I'm anxious to compare it with yours."

"By all means, let us do so."

They hastened downstairs once more, and Dr. Cumberland strode outside to his car, to return with a camphorwood chest which he carried with the greatest reverence.

He opened the chest, tenderly drew out a gray-violet vase.

"Ah!" cried Flora under her breath.

Dr. Cumberland placed his vase on the table beside that which already stood there. No question — the two were identical. He shook his head in a rapture of wonder and delight. "There, Mrs. Brewer, is a sight to set every Orientologist the world over mad with envy." His manner suddenly changed. He chewed at his lip. "But perhaps I am exaggerating. After all there are hundreds, possibly thousands of fine Sung vases in existence. These two are certainly good typical examples. In fact, Mrs. Brewer, I might be tempted to buy from you, should you feel so inclined. I can offer you," he considered craftily, "four thousand dollars."

Flora laughed contemptuously. "My dear Dr. Cumberland. You must be out of your mind. I value my vase a great deal higher."

"Ah yes? Exactly what value do you place on it?"

"At least ten thousand dollars."

Dr. Cumberland shook his head ruefully. "Mrs. Brewer, you have lived too long in the East. You are too harsh a bargainer. I can offer you — let us say, eight thousand?" And Dr. Cumberland drew a checkbook from his pocket.

Again Flora laughed, more coldly and metallically than ever. "I did not say that I would sell for ten thousand, I merely pointed out that ten thousand dollars is the minimum value of the vase." She looked slantingly sideways at him. "What would you say if I offered you eight thousand dollars for your vase?"

"My dear lady," said Dr. Cumberland reproachfully. "There is always a difference when one is buying and when one is selling. The minimum value of my vase is, as you quite correctly put it, at least ten thousand dollars."

Flora went to the table, inspected Dr. Cumberland's vase. She picked it up, scrutinized the potter's mark, frowned a trifle, compared it with the mark on the foot of her own vase. "Very well," she said, "I'll offer you ten thousand for yours."

Dr. Cumberland shook his head sadly. "I'm a collector, Mrs. Brewer. I abhor selling pieces which I love." He considered. "I have an idea. Let's do it the sporting way. We'll toss a coin. If I win, I'll buy from you at ten thousand; if I lose, you take my vase at ten thousand."

Flora shook her head. "No, Dr. Cumberland, definitely not."

Dr. Cumberland reached out to take his vase, then paused, "I can't conceivably induce you to sell your vase?"

"I'm afraid not."

"Then I'll have to sell to you. I can't bear to break up the set. But only on one condition."

"What is the condition, Dr. Cumberland?"

"That you allow me to visit occasionally, to feast my eyes on these two marvellous pieces standing side by side."

Flora nodded graciously. "I see no harm in that. If you will be kind enough to write me a bill of sale, I will draw you up a check."

Dr. Cumberland said dolefully, "Mrs. Brewer, once again, I urge you to reconsider. Think of the pleasure these vases could bring to the distinguished scholars of the world who regularly visit my exhibitions."

"You forget, Dr. Cumberland, that I too am a collector."

Dr. Cumberland threw up his hands in defeat. He drew out his notebook, wrote in a fury of haste. "There — the sooner it's over with the better."

"If you will come upstairs," said Flora, "I will draw up my check."

Dr. Cumberland took his check and departed. Flora gazed at her two vases with distended nostrils. Poor Dr. Cumberland — so young and so foolish. If each vase separately were worth ten thousand, the unique matched pair was easily worth fifty or sixty thousand. Flora chuckled, and examined the bill of sale Dr. Cumberland had written.

July 16, 1961
   Sold to Mrs. Flora Brewer for the sum of ten thousand dollars one vase, violet-gray in color, identical to that now in her possession.

The signature was almost indecipherable — a hasty scrawl which might be most anything.

"Heigh-ho," said Flora. "This is indeed a red-letter day."

That evening she telephoned Kendall, and triumphantly described the advantage she had taken of the brash young Dr. Cumberland.

Kendall seemed peculiarly skeptical. "Ten thousand dollars, eh? This Dr. Cumberland — what did he look like?"

Flora described him.

Kendall laughed shortly. "Did you meet a blonde young woman of twenty-one or twenty-two?"

"No," said Flora. "I did not. Why do you ask?"

"I fear you've been had."

"That's not possible. The Institute —" she paused. "Just a minute." She went to the vases, picked one of them up, then the other, held them to the light, squinted, frowned. "I'm sure you're quite wrong, Kendall. The vases are identical. I can't tell them apart." Her voice became reflective. "They do seem glossier — *newer*."

Kendall laughed — cynically and cruelly, so it seemed to Flora. "You've been had. And you know who's done it."

"Yes," said Flora, her teeth together. "I know... I know now."

CHAPTER XIV

THE RINGING OF THE TELEPHONE awoke Lulu. She lay quiet a moment, disinclined to move, although the morning sun slanted through her living room window and the clock beside her said half-past eight.

The telephone rang again, insistently. Not a nice sound, thought Lulu. Bad news.

She slid out of bed, limped on bare feet across the cold floor, picked up the telephone. "Hello?"

"Is this Luellen Enright?" spoke a crisp measured voice.

"Well, well," said Lulu flippantly. "Aunt Flora."

"This is Flora Brewer. I understand that you have my vase."

"Good heavens, Aunt Flora, what an odd thing to say!"

"No odder than the attendant circumstances. I assume that you thought you were playing a joke. In any case, I want the vase back immediately, and as for the check I gave that young man, please tear it up."

Lulu laughed. "Aunt Flora, you are marvellous. And indescribable. It's hard to fit an adjective to you."

"I'm afraid I don't understand you, Luellen. I take it that you will return the vase at once?"

"I don't believe I have any vase of yours," said Lulu. "In fact I'm sure I don't. Just my own vase, the one I brought from Onomichi."

Flora's voice became even crisper. "That is a question I don't intend to argue with you. Through some means which I still don't understand — I'm sure they were very clever; fraud and deceit are always clever — you managed to lay your hands on that vase and cheat me of a large sum of money. If both are returned by this evening, I will regard the entire matter as a joke, if in very poor taste."

"And if not?"

"I assure you that you'll find yourself in serious difficulties with the law."

"Yes," said Lulu. "I imagine that I will — if you can prove ownership."

"I have nothing more to say, Luellen. I will expect to see you some-time during the day."

The telephone went dead. Lulu shrugged, decided against going back to bed, and started a pot of coffee.

The doorbell rang. Lulu looked out the window, without haste slipped into a bathrobe, opened the door. "Home-coming day with the Brewers. What do you two want?"

"I believe we'd better come to an understanding," said Kendall.

"I just spoke to your mother," said Lulu. "She seems to have got up on the wrong side of the bed."

"Well?" said Kendall. "Do you want to talk here?"

"I don't want to talk at all," said Lulu. "If you insist on it, come in."

Kendall stepped firmly forward; Oliver, who had been lounging to the rear, followed with a quick side-glance at Lulu.

Kendall turned a quick fastidious look around the untidy living room, seated himself on the edge of the sofa. "There's no question but what you're clever. But you've gone too far. My mother is determined to sign a complaint against you. I persuaded her to hold off until Oliver and I could talk with you."

Oliver felt impelled to speak. "In short, we want our money back." He grinned sheepishly.

Lulu poured herself a cup of coffee, leaned back against the table. She sipped, considered Kendall and Oliver reflectively. "I must say that you Brewers certainly are impervious to shame. Aren't you embar-rassed coming in here like this?"

"It's a question of money," said Kendall coldly. "Whatever has hap-pened — and I assure you I haven't forgotten — has no bearing upon the dollars-and-cents issue. We want our money back or you'll be in trouble with the law."

"What can you prove?" She glanced contemptuously sidelong at Oliver. "You wouldn't dare bring charges against me."

"We're appealing to your better nature," suggested Oliver.

"Bah!" cried Kendall in a fury. "No such thing. I'm threatening you with prosecution."

Lulu laughed. "Go ahead, prosecute. Once you take me into court I can sell the story to a magazine. It's certainly good for a laugh. Three clever Brewers."

"But you cheated us," cried Oliver. "It's no better than stealing."

"How could I steal my own money?" asked Lulu. "You had no right to it in the first place."

"But we did," said Kendall. "You don't seem to appreciate the situation. You killed our father." He spoke with insulting distinctness. "Do you understand? You killed our father!"

"And we're entitled to damages!" chimed in Oliver.

"Whether a child or not," continued Kendall, "you committed the act. Why should we be penalized?"

"There's a certain degree of Stone Age logic to your position," said Lulu, "and it would be even more persuasive except for one small matter: I did not kill your father."

Kendall's eyebrows rose incredulously, Oliver cocked his head sideways. Kendall leaned a little forward. "You say you did not kill Father? You fired the shot!"

"I fired *a* shot," said Lulu. "He was coming toward me, the bullet must have gone into the dirt about six feet to the left of his feet. Your father died from a bullet in the back of the head."

Kendall sat slowly back in his chair.

"Amazing," said Oliver.

Kendall leaned suddenly forward. "This is ridiculous. If you didn't shoot Father, who did?"

Lulu sipped her coffee. "I wish I knew. He, or she, owes me nine years of childhood — nine years in that juvenile jail. For something I didn't do."

Kendall's face became pink and vaguely concerned. He looked uncertainly at Oliver, who bluffly pronounced a rude expletive. "All nonsense," said Oliver.

Kendall said slowly, "Of course it's nonsense…Why would anyone want to kill Father? Why —" he stopped short as Lulu smiled in cynical amusement.

"You would," said Lulu. "He was going to make you marry that girl. Oliver would. Your father was stopping off his desserts, big tragedy. Aunt Flora would. Uncle Maurice was acting in ways she disapproved of. Heaven only knows who else hated him."

Kendall stared at her fascinated. He licked his lips, gave his narrow head a jerk. "But you admit firing the shot. Isn't that a definite fact — more important than all this theory?"

"But I never hit him," said Lulu in a voice of sweet reason.

Oliver said suddenly, "I know how we could prove it. That little freak Chickweed. He used to sit in the window watching everything. If anything went on he'd see it."

Kendall frowned, made a slight sound in his throat, glanced sideways at Oliver. "All this puts a slightly different complexion on matters… Hmf… I suppose we can let sleeping dogs lie. All this happened so long ago. Well… I suppose we can concede to you the money left you by your father. But you'll have to return to us every cent over this amount. Or we'll take you to court."

"Ha!" said Lulu, pouring herself more coffee. "Have you never heard of compound interest? And costs of recovery? And wasted time? And Mental anguish, wear and tear on the nerves? You're getting off cheap. And now that you've brought up the matter — what happened to Chick?"

Oliver threw up his hands. "After that day we never saw him again. I heard he died."

"Poor little Chickie." She looked from one to the other. "You two were even more detestable then than you are now."

"Regardless of the bouquets," said Kendall tartly, "what about my money?"

"And mine? And our mother's vase?"

"When shrimps learn to whistle, as one of our foreign friends puts it, you shall have it."

Kendall and Oliver departed, muttering together as they went down the walk.

Lulu dressed swiftly in a neat gray suit, drove across the bridge, to San Francisco. She followed the Embarcadero past Fisherman's Wharf into the Marina, and presently parked on Sherwood Street. A single block downhill from Belvedere, with its fashionable mansions and green old gardens, Sherwood Street was unabashedly lower-middle class.

After five minutes peering up the hill to the rear elevations of the houses along Belvedere, Lulu fixed on 2528 Sherwood as the house she sought.

With heart beating fast she stepped into the little red-tiled mock-Spanish alcove, rang the doorbell.

The door swung back. A very large man of thirty, tall, massive, and flabby, stared somberly down at her. He wore gray-green trousers, a stained white T-shirt, which stretched mightily to cover his paunch. His face was pallid, his eyes large with sagging lids, his nose long, his mouth loose. All in all, thought Lulu, a most repulsive man. She said, "Excuse me, I'm trying to find a family who lived here about thirteen years ago. I wonder if—"

The man backed away, started to swing shut the door. "I've only been here a year."

"Do you own this house? Could you tell me whom you bought from?"

He shook his big head and his jowls swung. "Go talk to Cardini. Vic Cardini, he's the landlord."

"Where does he live?"

"Two, three houses up the street." The door shut in Lulu's face. Angrily she turned away. "Disgusting walrus of a man..." She went two houses up the street, rang the bell; a wizened little woman in a long black dress peered through a crack. "Whatcha want?"

"Does Mr. Cardini live here?"

"No." The door quickly closed. Lulu went to the next house, which had been recently painted a peculiarly odious yellow, and still exhaled oil and turpentine. At the ring of the bell the door opened. A portly white-haired man stood in the doorway, baby-pink face split in an affable grin. "Hello, hello," he called. "What's a pretty young gal want with an old man like me?"

"You're Mr. Cardini?"

"Yep, I been him for sixty years, I guess I keep on being him. Come on in, don't stand out in the cold; come on, come on, it's all right, I ain't gonna bother you. I'm too old now." Genial Mr. Cardini ushered Lulu in with a gallant gesture of his hand. The hall smelled rich of olive oil and garlic. Mr. Cardini noticed Lulu sniffing the air. "Smells good, eh? Eggplant with red sauce. You like some?"

"No, thanks," said Lulu. "What I came —"

Cardini held up a hand in mock dismay. "I know. You selling something. Insurance? I got lots of it. Books? I don't read much. I give money to the Community Chest, I can't give no more."

"No," said Lulu. "I'm not selling anything. I just wanted to ask you about your house up the street."

Cardini's eyes were like those of a clever parrot. They scrutinized her closely. "My house, eh? What about it? You want to live there? I kick out that pig that lives there now. Big man like that, you know what he does? Runs a cigar counter. Sells newspapers. He ought to be out fishing. I'm an old-time fisherman. That's a hard life."

Lulu said, "Do you remember the people who lived there about thirteen years ago?"

Cardini puckered up his old mouth thoughtfully. "That's a long time. What was their name?"

"That I don't know. I want to find the little boy who lived there then. He was sick."

"Yeah, yeah, I know who you mean." He stumped to a table, held up a bottle. "Maybe you like a glass of wine? This good wine. My nephew he makes it."

Lulu took a glass of wine and at Cardini's insistence followed him back to the kitchen, seated herself at the kitchen table, waited till Cardini looked cautiously inside the oven. "This gonna be good," said Cardini. "You hungry?"

"No, thanks," said Lulu. "About the people —"

"Yeah." Cardini nodded portentously. "I'm trying to think. Father was a garage mechanic, something like that. Little boy, he was sick. Look like a little white bird. Seems like they took him away somewhere."

"What was their name?"

Cardini drank some wine, shook his head. "I just don't remember. Smith? Jones? Lot of people name like that. An Italian name I remember."

"Do you have any rent receipts? Or a lease?"

"No. I never keep that stuff. Just gets in the way."

"Where did the father work?"

"He was a mechanic, I guess he worked in a garage. Pretty smart man, don't talk much. Not like me. I talk a lot, I'm dumb. But I'm good cook."

"You don't know what garage?"

Cardini gave his head a profound and definite shake. "I don't know."

"I wonder where I could find out where they are... Did they leave anything when they went? Books, papers, furniture? Luggage? Clothes?"

Cardini shook his head to each question. "Don't seem like they had much. Except the little boy — all kinds of toys and games. And things like bats and balls and fishing rods, and when he could hardly walk! What do you think of that? Funny, eh?"

"Was there a doctor who took care of the little boy?"

"I guess so. I don't look, I mind my own business. The tenants don't like it when you in, out, in, out all the time." Cardini spoke in a foolish falsetto, " 'You spill ink on the wall, my, my, what a mess! You let baby wet the floor, my, my, you should be more careful! You slam door too hard, my, my, you pull door off hinges.' " Cardini chuckled. "Naw, they don't like that."

"Did they have any friends in the neighborhood?"

"I don't know. I hardly see them, except for once or twice a month."

Lulu pondered. "What about utilities? Who paid them?"

"Me. That's in the rent."

"How about the telephone?"

"He paid that himself."

Lulu said, "I wonder if you'd let me call the business office and ask if they have any records."

"Sure, help yourself. You be my guest."

Lulu went to the telephone in the hall, called Operator and was connected to the business office. "I wonder if you could help me locate someone," said Lulu. "A family who lived thirteen years ago at 2528 Sherwood Street."

"I'm sorry," said the toneless voice. "We don't have that information available."

"But aren't there records? What about your old directories?"

"We don't list by the street numbers."

Lulu hung up, sat thinking. She looked in the directory, called the Auto Mechanics and Garage Worker's Union. "Thirteen years ago one of your members lived at 2528 Sherwood Street. Would there be any way of finding out his name? It's very important that I locate him."

"I'm sorry, ma'am. I just don't know how we'd go about finding out. We have thousands of members. I doubt if there'd be any record that long ago."

Lulu went glumly back into the kitchen. Mr. Cardini had set out two plates heaped with eggplant cooked with tomato and cheese, and was slicing a loaf of crusty bread. Without further ado Lulu sat down at the table.

"Can't find him, eh? You a lawyer, something like that? Pretty young to be a lawyer. You just a young girl. Me, I'm sixty, I ain't a lawyer; you ain't no lawyer."

"Quite true," said Lulu.

"You collect bills, eh? That's all right. I don't care. We all got to eat. Even bill collectors got to eat. How you like the eggplant? Pretty good, eh?"

"Yes," said Lulu, "it's very good. Not enough garlic, though."

Cardini stopped with fork half-raised to his mouth. "What you mean, not enough garlic? Lotsa garlic."

Lulu shook her head primly. "You can't cook garlic with eggplant with so much eggplant. And all that tomato."

Cardini chuckled. "This ain't garlic with eggplant, it's eggplant with garlic. See all that green stuff? That's basilica, fresh from the ground. Garlic with eggplant, hah!"

"It's really very good," said Lulu. "Too bad you can't remember as good as you cook."

"Yeah, too bad."

There was a moment or two of silence. Lulu suddenly stopped eating.

"Whatsa matter?" demanded Cardini. "Too much garlic? Or too much eggplant?"

"I was thinking that I'd like to get inside that house for a few minutes."

Cardini shook his big head. "Can't be done. Those people are funny. He's big fat slob, she's one of these religious maniacs. All the time in church, everywhere you look inside the house there's something with the church." He held up his fork. "You say my memory is no good. I tell you something. You see down the street, that little park? Hildreth Park, they call it. Well, the guy used to take his little boy down there every Sunday morning. He'd sit and play dominoes with the old-timers, and the little boy he'd sit and watch. Some of the guys been there for years, come down every nice day. You go down ask them, maybe they know."

Lulu scraped up the last of the eggplant, declined a further helping, allowed Cardini to clap her on the shoulder with a friendly hand, thanked him for wine, eggplant, garlic and information and departed.

At the curb she looked back toward 2528 Sherwood, and saw the tall paunchy man leave his house. He wore a loose black suit, a shapeless gray hat. As Lulu watched he lumbered off toward the bus stop with a peculiar rolling flourish of the hips.

Lulu hesitated, then turned and walked in the opposite direction toward Hildreth Park.

The time was now about eleven-thirty; Hildreth Park looked green and fresh. At tables in the central quadrangle a dozen games of chess, checkers, and dominoes were in progress. Lulu watched a moment, then approached a tall thin man in a neat tweed suit who had just risen from a game of dominoes.

"Excuse me," said Lulu, "I wonder if you would give me some information."

"I'll certainly try."

"About thirteen years ago a man used to come here Sunday mornings with his sick little boy and play dominoes. I wonder if there's anyone here who would remember him."

The thin man craned his neck, pointed. "See old Tige over there? That red-faced man in the brown jacket. Ask him."

Lulu went to the red-faced man in the brown jacket. He looked rough and ribald and good-natured; at Lulu's question he squinted in deep thought. He snapped his fingers. "I remember who you mean. Sick kid, you say."

"Yes. He was then about eleven."

Tige nodded. "Never said much, always looked tired. But with no wife and a sick kid, no wonder he was tired."

"Do you remember his name?" asked Lulu anxiously.

"I think we used to call him Zig. He had some kind of Slav name. Where's Old Slade? Not here. He's a 'ski, they used to talk together — Polack, or whatever. If anybody knew the man it was Slade."

"And where can I find Mr. Slade?"

"That I don't know. His first name is Alexander; he's probably in the telephone book."

"Thank you," said Lulu.

In a nearby telephone booth she looked up the name: 'Alexander Slade. MYrtle 4-6795 — 1935 Trevelyan Street'.

Lulu telephoned. No answer.

She left the booth in disgust, stood impatiently in the noonday sunshine, with seagulls from the bay wheeling overhead. Trevelyan Street was only a block distant; 1935 must be close at hand. She set off briskly, and five minutes later stood in front of 1935: a six-story apartment building. She examined the directory, pressed the button marked: #5 — A. Slade.

There was no answer. Lulu looked down the brass board: #6 — Margaret Nesbitt. She pressed the button; a calm voice asked, "Who's there, please?"

"I'm looking for Mr. Slade," said Lulu.

"He's in Apartment 5," said the voice, now cool and dry.

"Yes, I know, but he doesn't seem to be in. I wondered if you might know where I could find him."

"No, I'm afraid not. He's out a great deal, but where he goes I don't know."

"Oh blast," muttered Lulu.

The voice asked with rather caustic delicacy, "Is this a personal, or a commercial matter?"

"Personal," said Lulu hopefully. "Completely personal."

"I usually hear him when he comes in. Would you like me to give him a message?"

"Yes, by all means, if you'd be so kind. My name is Lulu Enright."

"How do you spell that?"

Lulu spelled her name. "My telephone number is TRaverse 6-1380. Would you have him call me as soon as possible? Any hour of the day or night."

"I'll give him your message," said the calm dry voice. "He's a heavy drinker and not too reliable, so you may or may not hear from him."

Lulu expressed her thanks, returned to her car, where she contemplated the house Professor Chickweed had inhabited so long ago. What had she learned? Nothing, really, that she had not already known... But the idea that she'd had before kept returning to her mind. Tantalizing... Lulu alighted from the car. The big-bellied man had gone, his wife would be at home. She paused to reflect, then turned back into her car, fumbled in the glove compartment, found a notebook. Carrying the notebook conspicuously, she marched across the sidewalk, across the red tiles of the pseudo-Spanish alcove, pressed the bell-button.

A moment passed, then the pleated lace which hung across the glass door stirred. The door opened and this time a young woman not much older than Lulu looked forth. She was thin-faced, with a tremulous mouth, brown hair turned up into rollers.

"Hello," said Lulu brightly. "I'm from the TV Popularity Poll. Do you watch TV?"

"Oh, yes," said the woman, with a spark of interest. "I'm a real fan."

"Oh fine! Our ratings determine which shows will be broadcast next year, and we interview very few families, as you probably know. Do you have a few minutes?"

"Well yes. I guess so."

Lulu moved confidently forward, the woman stepped back.

"My," said Lulu admiringly, "what a nice place you have here. I've never been in this house before, although when I was a little girl I used to know the people who lived here."

The woman looked at Lulu with a lacklustre display of polite interest. "Is that right? The world is such a small place, isn't it?"

"Yes, that's certainly true. And this is your TV set? It's very handsome."

"Yes," said the woman, "we went all out and got the best; it's such an important thing, really, we give so much of our time to it. Although I must say that I disapprove of many of the programs, if you know what I mean."

"Oh yes, I certainly do," said Lulu. "Of course I'm not supposed to comment about such things myself." She opened her notebook. "Your name is —"

"I'm Evelyn Degan. My husband's in the publishing business."

"That's an interesting line of work." Lulu looked around the room which was furnished in light green over-stuffed furniture. There was a pair of enormous lamps with lavender shades, and of course the television set. "I had no idea the house was like this inside. Of course I only knew the little boy who lived here, who was very sick. I used to live in the house just up the hill, and I'd talk to him by the hour while he sat in his window." Lulu jumped to her feet. "I wonder — would you think me absolutely terrible if I asked to see Chick's room? I've thought so much about the poor little waif over the years…"

Evelyn Degan said grudgingly, "I guess so…The room's a mess, we don't use it now except for — well, we just plain don't use it."

"I don't mind. Your house is ever so much neater than mine." Lulu purposefully started up the stairs.

"It's a real job keeping house," agreed Evelyn Degan, coming behind. "Men can't imagine what a woman goes through just keeping a place clean. My husband comes home, he likes a good meal on the table, and if it isn't just right I hear about it, believe me…This is our room to the front. I guess this must be the room you mean, looking over the back yard." She opened the door. Lulu went in, looked out the window. "Yes. This is it."

Memories, images. The garden had changed not at all: there were the two maples, the lawn, the side fences, overgrown with rose bushes. From this window Chick had seen the sun and the moon, and had watched the yellow-glowing windows of the Brewer house. Through this window had passed Purr, treading a meager ledge of roof twenty feet above the concrete. The lawn beyond the fence had been like a stage for Chick, where three children had walked: Kendall, Oliver, and Lulu…Where was Chick now? What had he seen from the window?

Lulu looked around the room, now used for the storage of miscellaneous household appurtenances. The bed was gone; all Chick's pictures and trophies were gone; the walls were bare.

Lulu fell to her knees. Evelyn Degan stared in wonderment. "Excuse me," said Lulu, "I must pray. For the soul of the little boy who lived in this room and is now dead." She bent her head, and spoke under her breath. Evelyn Degan watched aimlessly and uncomfortably a moment, then walked back and forth fidgeting.

"I'm sorry to take your time," said Lulu, "but if you're a religious person you surely know the power of prayer."

"That's very true," said Evelyn Degan. She went reluctantly to the door. "I'll be downstairs; you can come down whenever you're finished." She departed.

Lulu listened, and heard Evelyn's feet dubiously descending the stairs. She jumped up, ran to the window. The secret panel, would it still press back? And in the hiding place... She pushed. The panel eased back. Her hand met solidity. She drew out the heavy cold object: a movie camera. She reached into the gap again: the Book of Dreams, thirteen years hidden from view. And where was Chick, that he had failed to return for a trove so precious?

Lulu came down the stairs. "Mrs. Degan!"

Evelyn's head popped out of the kitchen. "Yes?" Her voice was cool.

"I'm really not myself today. May we postpone the interview?"

Evelyn sniffed. "Certainly, if you don't feel good."

"Thank you very much," said Lulu. "You're very understanding."

Back in her car Lulu opened her purse, withdrew the camera. She looked at the film index window, rubbed away the dust of years. Forty-two feet of film had been exposed. Lulu chewed her lip thoughtfully. What happened to film when it remained thirteen years in the camera?

She put the camera down, turned to look at the Book of Dreams. Carefully, diffidently, she took it into her hands. The cover was as she remembered it, the title printed in red letters with black outlines, surrounded by green vines on which bloomed purple and blue flowers.

Much love had gone into this book, thought Lulu. Chick had lavished love on his Book of Dreams... She hesitated, then slowly turned back the crackling covers. Neatly written paragraphs, dated. A map — of where? Of no region Lulu recognized: a mythical kingdom, with rivers and mountains, villages, towns and the capital city Waldemar. Here were the Tartary Woods, there Dragonfire Castle, and beyond The Wild Waste... Lulu turned the page, to find a sketch of Dragonfire

Castle, sprawled on a sullen crag with pine trees behind. Opposite stood a number of stiffly drawn figures in carefully detailed uniforms, variously labeled: 'Herald', 'Butler', 'Knight in Court Dress', 'Varlet', 'Page', 'Swordsman'.

On the pages following Chick had begun a romance, describing the adventures of young Sir Mervyn, the evil Lord Chastain, Princess Valisande, wizards, witches, knights by the dozen. He had completed two chapters, before halting in mid-page. In the blank space at the bottom Chick, evidently in a playful mood, had written, "My dear friend, Prince Purkin of Catfish Castle, came to call today, bearing as a gift a dozen chests of the finest cockleburrs." And below, "Princess Valisande: she is a girl delicate and graceful and sad, with beautiful yellow hair. The ogres who guard her are called Kendool and Oliphant, and are both ugly and fearsome. Her real name is Valisande, but her dear friends call her Lulu, which is a cute name they use for short."

Lulu turned on through the Book of Dreams, her mouth curved and twisting. At a poem entitled 'Ode to Purkin' she paused to read:

> Purkin would not chase a rat,
> Purkin is a gentle-cat.
> Purkin never spills the cream,
> Of such a crime he'd never dream.
> Purkin holds his tail on high
> And looks the whole world in the eye.
> I pray that Purkin won't grow old
> And never starves or catches cold
> Because he's worth his weight in gold.

At this point, so it seemed, Chick had commenced to keep a daily record of events, in diary form. Lulu glanced down the entries, comprehending some but not all of the allusions.

> Today we drove to Sausalito, where there are beautiful boats. When I get well, I will build a boat and sail all over the world. Purkin will be ship's cat and wear a blue jacket. Tomorrow is Sunday, and I suppose we will go to the park and play dominoes. I can

beat almost everyone there. My leg feels very well today. I hope I am getting better.

Another entry was written with wild and almost hysterical strokes of the pen.

Today my dear friend, Prince Purkin of Catfish Castle, engaged in valorous combat with the beast-men of Tenigor Keep, and only by help of the magic Princess could he escape with his life. Prince Purkin is scared and miserable, and when I become strong and mighty I will hurt and scare the beast-men as they scared and hurt Prince Purkin.

Another entry, almost the last.

Today is my birthday. I don't feel very well, but I have a new camera. My father bought me film and has showed me how to use the camera. When we go camping I will take: 1. Camera, 2. Gun, 3. Fishing rod, 4. Compass, 5. Pocket knife, 6. Wristwatch. I would like Lulu to come too. I hate Kendall and Oliver, they act as if they owned the entire world. If they —

The entry inexplicably halted. Then, the last entry in the Book of Dreams.

June 10. A beautiful sunny day, and I am outside. Lulu is looking through the fence and I am writing. She is unhappy, and I can understand why, living with Kendall and Oliver. I am watching Purr. I think I will take him inside, and bring out my camera. I will take some pictures of Lulu.

And there was no more.

Lulu looked at the camera lying on the seat beside her. Enigmatic black box, containing secrets of life and death... A face was looking in to the car from the sidewalk, a face contorted and angry: Evelyn Degan. "What did you take from my house? You're not a research person!

You're a thief!" And Evelyn Degan backed away, hand to her pallid face, aghast at her own words. She looked up and down the sidewalk. "I should call the police!"

Lulu started the car. With heart pounding she drove off down Sherwood Street. In the rear-view mirror Evelyn Degan became a miniature faceless shape in a green dress, jerking and gesticulating, which finally disappeared.

Lulu returned across the bridge, drove to Berkeley, parked in front of a camera shop. Taking the camera, she went in, and presently one of the clerks attended her. "Can I help you?"

Lulu displayed Professor Chickweed's camera. "Yes. You can. There's film in this camera, exposed thirteen years ago. Can I have it developed now?"

The clerk cocked his head dubiously to the side. "I doubt if anything will show up…To tell you the truth, I don't quite know…" He consulted his associate, who looked similarly doubtful. "Maybe using some real dynamite-type developer, you might get an image, if the film holds together. Certainly no quality job."

"Who could do it for me? Immediately?"

There were shrugs. "Immediately — how soon is that?"

"Now."

More shrugs and disinterest. "The commercial laboratories take at least two days."

"But isn't there someone who can process the film right now?"

"You might try Harry Coleman, on Acton Street. He does custom work."

Lulu noted the address, departed the camera shop.

Chapter XV

Harry Coleman at the photo laboratory seemed so absurdly young, so fair and fresh-shaven and innocent, that Lulu felt a qualm as she handed him the camera.

"Please," she said, "be very careful."

He smiled politely, but promised nothing. Heart pounding with anxiety, Lulu watched him take the camera into the back room. After an interminable wait, he returned, carrying a spool. Lulu, searching his face, saw the same calm polite smile. "Did it — turn out?"

The technician pursed his lips judiciously. "Not well. The image is blurred, and I don't think the photographer was really experienced —"

"But there's a picture?"

"Oh yes. There's a picture."

"Can I look at it?"

"Certainly. Right over here, at this little editing machine."

He looped the film over the sprockets, turned a switch. Lulu stared into the bright flickering lens, leaned closer. The film went blank. "Can I see it once more?"

Once more the shores of time receded, and the little figures, alive and yet not alive, performed acts which were real and yet gone forever.

"Thank you," said Lulu in a muffled voice. "Thank you very much. You've done a wonderful job."

She drove slowly to her flat, parked, turned off the engine, sat several minutes in the car, then slowly opened the door and wandered down the walk. Once inside, she sank down on the sofa, with knees folded under her, gazed unseeingly out the window, across the untended little garden. The room was warm and quiet, Lulu stared down the avenues of recollection, and the past was as real as the present. At last she turned her head, looked over the little reel of film. "What shall I do?" she muttered. "What shall I do?"

The telephone jangled sharply; Lulu jumped to her feet, then slowly crossed the room. "Hello?"

"This is Kendall Brewer."

"Oh," said Lulu. "Kendall. What do you want?"

Kendall spoke, but Lulu's attention had wandered. Kendall's voice seemed blurred, and the words conveyed no meaning. Finally she interrupted. "What are you saying? I didn't hear you."

"In essence," came Kendall's voice, resonant with righteous purpose, "I have been asking you if you are willing to meet with us. We wanted to sign a complaint, but Mr. McHugh prevailed upon us to make one last attempt —"

"Who's Mr. McHugh?"

"Are you listening?" Kendall demanded sharply. "Mr. McHugh is the District Attorney. He is taking a personal interest in this case, and I think that you'd be very wise to —"

"Just what is it you want, Kendall?"

"I want you to meet with us, and listen to what Mr. Goble has to say."

"And who is Mr. Goble?"

"An assistant to the District Attorney. He feels, as I do, that —"

"I don't care what either of you feel. I really don't care to talk to you."

Kendall's voice came sharp and harsh. "I'll tell you what's going to happen if you don't see us; you're going back to jail where you belong."

Lulu laughed weakly. "Very well, Kendall. Since you insist."

"We'll be there in half an hour."

The line went dead. Lulu stood thinking, head bowed, fingers abstractedly turning the telephone dial. She made up her mind, lifted the receiver, dialed a number.

A familiar voice responded. "Hello."

"This is Lulu. Please, will you locate a movie projector somewhere and bring it over, right away?"

"A movie projector? What for?"

"I want to show some film to the Brewers."

"Very well," said Robert tonelessly. "What is it, eight millimeter? Or sixteen?"

"Eight."

"I'll be there as soon as possible."

"Rent one. Borrow one. Buy one. Only get it here — for sure."

"This all sounds rather mysterious."

"Yes," said Lulu. "Everything's been very mysterious — up till this afternoon."

"I'll be there," said Robert. The line went dead.

Lulu went to the bathroom, brushed her hair. She examined her reflection — a pale pretty face with loose blonde hair, eyes that seemed bright with too much intelligence — and tried to remember the round doubtful little countenance of thirteen years before. She laughed sadly. "I'll start everything all over. I'll forget everything. I'll become a new person. Because now things will be settled and done with — forever."

She returned to the living room, looked around with dissatisfaction, and prompted by some deep-seated feminine instinct, set about ordering the room.

A large black car slid softly up in front of the apartment house. Inside sat four persons. Lulu watched through the window. They were talking together volubly, almost heatedly.

The two in front — Kendall and a tall, heavily-built man in gray — left the car; the two in the rear remained. Kendall and the man in gray marched up the walk. Kendall pressed the button with a truculent finger. Lulu heaved a deep sigh, went to the door, opened it. "Come in."

Kendall nodded stiffly. "This is Mr. Clyde Goble, Assistant District Attorney."

Lulu acknowledged the introduction, drew back; the two men came cautiously into the room. Goble examined Lulu appreciatively. "You don't look like a desperate criminal, Miss Enright."

"I'm not desperate, at least," said Lulu.

"This is far out of my line, adjudicating family disputes — but as I heard the story from Mrs. Brewer, it seemed that the best interests of everyone, including the District Attorney's Office, could be served by an informal settlement."

"I agree," said Lulu. "When I first learned that the Brewers had decided to steal my money —"

"Let's keep the record straight," said Kendall in a bleak voice. "It was not your money. A certain sum was conveyed to my mother to use as she thought best — to help pay expenses. When you killed my father, the money was used to recompense us for our loss, and the hardships we suffered."

Lulu laughed scornfully. "You and Oliver look as if you'd suffered. Incidentally, why don't Oliver and Aunt Flora come inside? Are they bashful? Or ashamed of themselves?"

Kendall's skin became faintly pink. "Neither."

"Please have them come inside. Mr. Goble wants us to be friendly and informal. They're sitting out there like carcasses in the back of a butcher's truck, and after all —"

"There's no need to confuse the issue," snapped Kendall. "You swindled us — very artfully, I agree, but nevertheless you swindled us. If you return the money and my mother's vase we won't press charges, which I consider is charitable of us. That's our basic position, and I don't think we mean to alter it."

"I really think everyone should come in," said Lulu. "There are one or two other circumstances — side issues, perhaps, but since we're all together for the first time in thirteen years —"

Goble's patience had worn thin. He glanced fretfully at his watch. "Surely you can tell us whether or not you want to come to a reasonable settlement."

Lulu leaned back on the couch, examined the tips of her toes. "Matters are more complicated than you think, Mr. Goble. For instance — Kendall asserts that I shot my uncle. This is a falsehood."

Kendall snorted. "You don't seriously —"

"I can very easily demonstrate what happened."

Goble regarded her steadily for a moment. "Are you suggesting accidental death — or —" he hesitated.

"Bah!" said Kendall in disgust. "I hope, Mr. Goble, that you recognize a red herring when you see one."

"This is all very confusing," Goble admitted.

"I'll show you a red herring," said Lulu. "I'll show you some red faces too. But —" she turned to Goble "— shouldn't we have everybody concerned present?"

"I can't see any reason why they shouldn't be here." Goble turned reluctantly to Kendall. "It might be best, after all, to bring your mother and your brother in; the matter seems to be a bit involved."

"There'll only be wrangling," argued Kendall. "We came to settle a single issue —"

"But there's a dead man to be considered," said Lulu softly. "Your father."

Goble swung around, marched out to the car. After a moment or two of earnest conversation, he returned up the walk preceded by Oliver and Flora. Lulu anxiously looked up and down the street. Where was Robert?

Flora came into the room, nodded stiffly at Lulu, seated herself without words in the chair which Goble took it upon himself to bring forward. She inspected the room with a single swift comprehensive glance and thereupon held her eyes fixed upon Lulu.

"Very well," said Goble, drawing a deep breath. "I think we're all here now, and I hope we can clear up this whole unhappy mess."

Lulu turned one last glance out the window. No Robert. She went to her desk with as confident an air as possible, brought forth an envelope which she handed to Goble. "This is a letter from my father. I'd like you to read it."

Goble glanced through the letter, frowned, returned it uneasily into the envelope. "Naturally I can't pass judgments or render any verdicts, but it's certainly a fact that the courts tend to protect the rights of children when the intent of the parent is clear."

"And what do the courts do in regard to proved felonies?" demanded Flora sharply. "Do they encourage theft, extortion, the most underhanded and disgraceful acts imaginable?"

"The right of a person to reclaim his own property is recognized," said Goble. "Provided that he commits no breach of the peace in the process. Whether Miss Enright is innocent or guilty in this regard is not for me to decide." His voice took on a harassed note. "Please remember I came here not to decide the relative merits of two positions, but to help you reconcile your differences."

"Under the circumstances," said Kendall, "I don't think we care to reconcile differences. This young woman has committed a number of illegalities. We want restitution or we prosecute, it's as simple as that."

"Well said, Kendall," declared Flora. She intensified her gaze upon Lulu. "I want my vase, and I want it at once."

Goble looked at Lulu curiously. "What of this other matter? Do you have anything to tell us? Or —"

Lulu looked desperately out the window. Where, oh where, was Robert? It's been such a long time since I telephoned him... Improvise, temporize.

Flora rose to her feet. She was wearing a handsome suit of dark gray sharkskin, with a puff of lavender organdy at the throat; absently Lulu noted that the passage of thirteen years had touched Flora very lightly. Her skin was fine and milky, her hair as dark and carefully coiled as ever. Flora said, "I see no point in wasting any more time."

"Just a minute," said Lulu. "There's the matter of Uncle Maurice's death. You say I killed him, and therefore don't deserve to have my own money. Is that right?"

Flora gazed at her with stony indifference. "Not right, but close enough."

"I want to show I had nothing to do with the death of Uncle Maurice." If only Robert would show up. Lulu drew a deep breath. "I suppose you remember the little boy who lived in the house down the hill."

Oliver chuckled. "Professor Chickweed."

"I've been looking for Chick. No one seems to know what's happened to him. But on his birthday he was given a movie camera —"

The window darkened as a figure passed in front of it; Lulu ran to the door. "Robert! Where have you been!"

Robert held up the projector. "I had to run all over town for this contraption. I hope it works."

"I hope so too. You're just in time. Hang up a sheet."

Kendall asked, "Just what are you doing?"

"I'm going to show a movie," said Lulu, feeling suddenly fluid and almost giddy. "An old silent melodrama, produced by a certain Professor Chickweed. The actors are all amateur, they all play themselves — turning in excellent performances by the way. Robert, where are you?"

"I don't know where you keep the sheets."

"I'll get one. You pull the shades and plug in the projector."

"This is ridiculous," said Kendall in disgust. "I'm leaving."

"Suit yourself. But you'll miss a great production. Although technically the film is very poor. It was developed just today. The man used something he called 'dynamite'. There are blurs and spots and streaks — but I'm sure we'll all be entertained."

"Get on with it."

Lulu turned on the projector; a beam of white light stabbed toward the sheet which Robert had hung at the end of the room. "Let me give Mr. Goble some background. Professor Chickweed — no one seems to know his name — lived in the house overlooking the yard where Uncle Maurice was shot. He suffered from some sort of bone disease, probably pernicious anemia as well. He was very frail, and found it hard to walk. Kendall and Oliver whiled away otherwise boring hours by tormenting Professor Chickweed and his little cat."

"Get on with your movie," said Oliver in a tired voice.

Lulu began to thread the film. "The day the film was made started off very unpleasantly. I recall this quite clearly. Kendall, by some means he did not clearly understand, had put a girl in the family way. The girl wanted to get married, but Flora and Kendall rejected the idea. Uncle Maurice insisted on it, stating that it was a custom in the Brewer family. Oliver was also in the doghouse. He was repulsively fat, and Uncle Maurice had forbidden the dear little cherub all puddings, pies, custards, candies, and jellies. Oliver thought that the world had come to an end. Aunt Flora and Uncle Maurice were also having other differences, in connection with me."

Flora hissed something between her teeth.

"Get on with it then," said Oliver in a bored voice. "We'll call names in our own turn soon enough."

"The film is probably faked," said Kendall.

Lulu politely disagreed. "I don't think so. As a matter of fact there's a witness to verify its authenticity."

Oliver laughed easily. "Professor Chickweed?"

"Professor Chickweed is a figure of mystery," agreed Lulu. "No one seems to know what happened to him. But I imagine that Mr. Goble will make it his business to find out."

"Let's see the film," said Goble shortly.

"Very well. Robert, lights out. This is the first and last roll of film Professor Chickweed shot through his birthday camera."

The room went gray, with only the wan seep of dusk entering past the curtains. Against the sheet snapped a startling beam of light, creating a polychrome rectangle across which amorphous shapes shifted and blurred.

Oliver snickered nervously, became still as Lulu focused the image. On the window sill stood Purkin the cat. He paused, arched his back, rubbed his cheek delicately on the jamb, then abruptly jumped down into the obscurity of the room. Cut! And there was Purkin lapping milk from a bowl in a square of sunshine. He looked up, swung a pink tongue around his lips in relish, returned to his milk. Cut! A quick snatch of Purkin leaping through the window, out on the roof. The camera moved forward, out the window, followed Purkin as he walked away. Now — a dazzle of orange and yellow as an area of sun-struck film moved past the camera, followed by an eye-wrenching flutter of black objects swinging around a blue sky.

"I think Chick was trying to photograph a seagull," said Lulu. "But branches and trees and houses interfered." The scene abruptly became steady. There was the lawn, the green bluer than actuality. A little girl in a pink dress stood to one side, watching two boys who stood looking up into the maple tree.

"That's me," said Lulu. "Kendall and Oliver have successfully reduced Chick to tears, and now they seem to be planning mischief upon Chick's cat." The film sputtered in black, brown and yellow blurs. "I made them stop, the wretched little beasts; I threatened them with Kendall's gun. They ran to their father." The image came bright and clear. "And here he comes — good old Uncle Maurice. He's not averse to laying his hands on me."

An indignant sound from Flora. "Stop this insulting display."

No one paid her any heed.

"Here comes the good part," said Lulu. "Uncle Maurice is really not a nice man. You can't see too clearly — now you can. That's my bare bottom he's paddling… Now I run away… Watch now. Here's where I'm supposed to kill Uncle Maurice."

On the screen the little girl in the pink dress, staggering back, picked up the gun, and even as she lifted it, it jerked with a soundless report. Maurice, approaching, threw up his hands in surprise. The little girl flung down the gun, ran blindly up the lawn.

"Notice," said Lulu softly. "Uncle Maurice looks after her. He isn't feeling well, but he hasn't been shot. That's obvious. Uncle Maurice is feeling very badly. Apparently he's having a heart attack. Excitement, guns, spankings — hard on the ticker.

"There goes Uncle Maurice. He's sitting down on the bench, he's collapsing on the lawn." The scene shifted slightly. "Chick, of course, is enthralled by the wonderful movies he's making... Now, here comes someone very sinister." Lulu fell silent.

Flora came down the lawn. She saw the outstretched figure of Maurice, ran forward on quick little feet. She bent over, seemed to shake Maurice's shoulder, though here the picture was obscure. She stood erect, a trick of the sunlight throwing her handsome head into sudden sharp brightness. Her nostrils were distended, her motions quick and birdlike. She looked to right, to left, up the path.

"Is Maurice dead?" asked Lulu softly. "He doesn't move. Perhaps we can't see. Flora hardly wants to nurse an invalid. And she really doesn't approve of Maurice; he's been such a trial of late. In fact —" Flora gracefully leaned over, picked up the gun.

She held it to the prone body with a dramatic, almost Victorian flourish. The gun jerked.

"Oof," came Oliver's expiration of breath.

"Good Lord," muttered Kendall.

"Maurice is dead now," said Lulu.

Kendall sprang to his feet, walked toward the projector. Goble and Robert loomed in front of him. The image blurred, toppled off the screen. Lulu clicked off the motor.

"Stop this farce," cried Kendall. "Surely you can see what she's doing? She's tricking us! It's a faked picture."

"If it is," said Goble in a hollow voice, "she's done a remarkable job."

Flora stirred. Her voice was only a trifle hoarser than usual. "This is nonsense. It's libellous. I merely took up the gun."

"And it went off," suggested Lulu.

"I deny it. If you assert that the gun went off, I shall sue you for slander."

"Obvious trickery," muttered Kendall in an uncertain voice.

"Let's look at that bit again," said Goble.

Lulu backed off the film, restarted the motor. All eyes riveted on the screen. Once again Flora came down the garden, looked right, left, up the walk, leaned over the body, picked up the gun, then — with a delicate flourish as if she were playing croquet — pointed the gun to the back of Maurice's neck.

The telephone rang in the kitchen. Lulu stepped through the door, responded. To the subdued obligato of Lulu's voice the film continued. Flora put down the gun, thoughtfully picked up the cartridge... Something seemed to have caught her attention. She backed up a pace, looked across the fence, up, directly into the camera. For ten seconds the cold eyes stared up, and seemed to look across the years, through the screen, and deep into the soul of everyone in the room. Then, still looking up, softly and quietly she walked toward the back fence. Abruptly the screen went white. The film clicked emptily, along the sprockets.

"There's nothing more," said Lulu, who had returned to the room.

"This is a serious matter," said Goble, watching Flora from the corner of his eye. "Very serious indeed. We must find this, ah, Professor Chickweed."

"I've found him," said Lulu. She turned on the lights, pallid faces blinked at each other, avoiding direct contact with one ice-cold countenance. "That was Mr. Alexander Slade on the telephone. He knew Professor Chickweed very well. His real name was Steven Hovic. At noon on Sunday, June 10, 1948, he fell from the window of his bedroom to the concrete deck twenty feet below. He broke two collarbones, his pelvis and his back, and died at St. Mary's Help Hospital the same evening."

A silence more oppressive than sound occupied the room. Time passed — five seconds, ten seconds. Then everyone moved at the same time — slight shiftings of the hands and feet, furtive easings of position. Kendall and Oliver suddenly looked haggard and miserable.

"Good Lord," said Kendall huskily. "This is awful." He looked fleetingly at Oliver, then turned his eyes to the wall.

Flora gathered herself. "What's awful about it?" she demanded in a voice like the tone of a cornet. "These imputations, these hints and innuendoes: they're not only false and insulting, they're — disgraceful."

Goble said to Lulu, "This man — his name is what?"

"Alexander Slade. His address is 1935 Trevelyan Street."

"He's sure of his facts?"

"Absolutely sure. He said that he was with Chick's father when they found Chick. He was in great pain, and could say nothing intelligible."

Kendall drew a deep breath. "There's still not a jot of any real evidence behind these accusations. And the only witness who could authenticate this very questionable film seems to have fallen to his death."

Lulu shook her head sadly. "No, Kendall...There's something in the film you failed to see. I'll run it through once more."

She rewound the spool. Flora rose to her feet. "I don't intend to stay another moment in this house."

Goble said courteously, "Please, Mrs. Brewer, I think it best that you wait just a bit longer. This is a very serious matter, and we can't just pretend that the implication of what we've seen doesn't exist."

"Now watch," said Lulu. Again the figures stalked quietly through the now grotesque patterns of Chick's melodrama. "Right here. Notice up there at the back door? See that white blur? It's somebody's face. Somebody was watching from the back porch. There — again...Just that little flicker."

"Nonsense," said Kendall. "Who could it be? It certainly wasn't me."

"It wasn't me," declared Oliver bluffly. "That film is so old it's falling to pieces. Full of spots."

"Something I was wondering about the other day," said Lulu. "Giorgio, the house-boy. In the old days the servants would stay a week and then they couldn't stand it any more. Giorgio's been there thirteen years. I wonder if there's any connection."

Flora sprang to her feet. "This is too much. Kendall, drive me home."

Goble said to Lulu, "May I use your phone?"

"Yes," said Lulu wearily.

"Who do you intend to call?" demanded Kendall.

"The San Francisco Police Department, naturally," said Goble. "I think they'll want a word with Giorgio."

Oliver had sidled across the room. Now he took a casual step toward the projector. Robert interposed himself. He and Oliver looked eye to eye a moment. Then Oliver turned and walked out the door. Flora followed, walking slowly, stiffly. Kendall turned to follow.

"Mr. Brewer," said Goble.

Kendall hesitated. "Yes?"

"Where are you going now?"

"Home, naturally."

"I suggest that you stay with your mother. Sometimes, under pressure of unexpected events, people have, well, had accidents which might have been avoided."

"Utterly ridiculous!" Kendall declared fiercely. He turned and strode from the apartment.

CHAPTER XVI

FLORA BREWER WAS CHARGED with the murder of Maurice Brewer, and in addition — for tactical reasons — the murder of Steven Hovic. At the trial her attorney energetically attacked the authenticity of the photographs offered in evidence by the prosecution.

The prosecution elicited testimony from two criminologists, a technician from the Eastman Kodak Corporation, and Harry Coleman, who had developed the film, to the effect that the film was a faithful record of events which had taken place on Sunday, June 10, 1948.

The prosecution suffered a setback when Giorgio Asuncion, houseboy to Flora Brewer for thirteen years, could not be located. It was generally assumed that Flora had sent him to Mexico or possibly the Philippine Islands. Another, more sinister, speculation was current. It could not be verified. Giorgio Asuncion, living or dead, was seen no more in San Francisco.

The prosecution called Alexander Slade to the stand. He testified that at noon on June 10, 1948, the day of Steven Hovic's death, he had called at 2528 Sherwood Street, in order to drive Steven to Hildreth Park. Approaching the house, he had noticed a woman coming down the walk which led to the back yard. He had never seen the woman before, but her appearance had made an indelible impression upon his memory: especially when five minutes later he found the boy writhing upon the concrete. He described the woman and her clothes to the detectives: clothes and woman matched the Flora Brewer of the photographs. In a line-up of eleven women he identified Flora Brewer without hesitation.

The jury found Flora Brewer guilty of the murder of Maurice Brewer, but entertained reasonable doubts in the case of Steven Hovic.

Flora Brewer was sent to Tehachapi State Prison for the remainder of her natural life.

A day or so later Lulu was approached by a representative of the Japanese Consul, who politely inquired after the Sung vase. This article had been stolen from the Imperial Treasury, he stated; nevertheless the Japanese Government was prepared to offer a substantial honorarium for its safe return. Lulu asked how high he was willing to go, and a figure of eighty-five hundred dollars was settled upon.

The vase was delivered to the Japanese Consul and Lulu received a check upon the San Francisco office of the Bank of Tokyo.

"With all this wealth," said Lulu to Robert, "we're foolish to stay here. Every day ships leave for exotic ports, and we should be aboard one of them."

Robert demurred. "I can't spend any of that money. It cost too much. Nine years of your childhood."

"Nothing of the sort," declared Lulu. "The money is an inheritance, and without your help I'd have had nothing at all."

Robert sadly shook his head. Lulu reminded him of the marriage at Reno: the money could be regarded as community property.

"Marriage?" retorted Robert scornfully. "With a faked license, a fake bride-groom?"

"A legal marriage, nevertheless," said Lulu. "Or so I think. We'll be married again, more formally, of course."

"Do you really want me for a husband?" Robert asked, "A cheat, a swindler?"

"I'm no better," said Lulu. "And anyway, we'll never cheat or swindle again, unless it becomes necessary."

Robert laughed. "Very well, Lulu. You've talked me into it."

"You're a hard case, Robert." Lulu heaved a deep sigh. "I was beginning to wonder about — well, my personal magnetism."

"It exists."

"That's settled then." She took both of his hands in hers. "Where shall we go? East? West? North? South? The world extends in all directions."

"Let's get aboard a freighter and see where it takes us."

"That's a good idea…" She sighed again. "It's wonderful to be so happy. Poor Aunt Flora, looking out from between the bars."

"Poor Aunt Flora."

"I don't think she ever allowed herself to recognize what she'd done. I fired the gun, I ran away; in Aunt Flora's mind, I was guilty. Looking at Chick's film — it must have been like remembering a bad dream." She laughed nervously. "But it's over with. I don't want to think of it anymore. Let's go look at freighters."

JACK VANCE was born in 1916 to a well-off California family that, as his childhood ended, fell upon hard times. As a young man he worked at a series of unsatisfying jobs before studying mining engineering, physics, journalism and English at the University of California Berkeley. Leaving school as America was going to war, he found a place as an ordinary seaman in the merchant marine. Later he worked as a rigger, surveyor, ceramicist, and carpenter before his steady production of sf, mystery novels, and short stories established him as a full-time writer.

His output over more than sixty years was prodigious and won him three Hugo Awards, a Nebula Award, a World Fantasy Award for lifetime achievement, as well as an Edgar from the Mystery Writers of America. The Science Fiction and Fantasy Writers of America named him a grandmaster and he was inducted into the Science Fiction Hall of Fame.

His works crossed genre boundaries, from dark fantasies (including the highly influential *Dying Earth* cycle of novels) to interstellar space operas, from heroic fantasy (the *Lyonesse* trilogy) to murder mysteries featuring a sheriff (the Joe Bain novels) in a rural California county. A Vance story often centered on a competent male protagonist thrust into a dangerous, evolving situation on a planet where adventure was his daily fare, or featured a young person setting out on a perilous odyssey over difficult terrain populated by entrenched, scheming enemies.

Late in his life, a world-spanning assemblage of Vance aficionados came together to return his works to their original form, restoring material cut by editors whose chief preoccupation was the page count of a pulp magazine. The result was the complete and authoritative *Vance Integral Edition* in 44 hardcover volumes. Spatterlight Press is now publishing the VIE texts as ebooks, and as print-on-demand paperbacks.

Colophon

This book was printed using Adobe Arno Pro as the primary text font, with NeutraFace used on the cover.

This title was created from the digital archive of the Vance Integral Edition, a series of 44 books produced under the aegis of the author by a worldwide group of his readers. The VIE project gratefully acknowledges the editorial guidance of Norma Vance, as well as the cooperation of the Department of Special Collections at Boston University, whose John Holbrook Vance collection has been an important source of textual evidence.

Special thanks to R.C. Lacovara, Patrick Dusoulier, Koen Vyverman, Paul Rhoads, Chuck King, Gregory Hansen, Suan Yong, and Josh Geller for their invaluable assistance preparing final versions of the source files.

Digitize: Richard Chandler, Joel Hedlund, Thomas Rydbeck; Format: R.C. Lacovara; Diff: Patrick Dusoulier, Damien G. Jones; Tech Proof: Donn Olmsted Sr; Text Integrity: Linnéa Anglemark, Patrick Dusoulier, Paul Rhoads; Implement: Derek W. Benson, Chris Reid; Security: Paul Rhoads; Compose: John A. Schwab; Comp Review: Christian J. Corley, John A. D. Foley, Paul Rhoads, Robin L. Rouch; Update Verify: Top Changwatchai, Marcel van Genderen, Bob Luckin, Paul Rhoads, Robin L. Rouch; RTF-Diff: Bill Schaub; Textport: Patrick Dusoulier, Charles King; Proofread: Ian Allen, Michel Bazin, Robert Collins, Andrew Edlin, Rob Friefeld, Rob Knight, R.C. Lacovara, Betty Mayfield, Turlough O'Connor, Errico Rescigno, Mike Schilling, Luk Schoonaert, Dave Worden

Artwork (maps based on original drawings by Jack and Norma Vance):

Paul Rhoads, Christopher Wood

Book Composition and Typesetting: Joel Anderson

Art Direction and Cover Design: Howard Kistler

Proofing: Christian J. Corley, Patrick Dusoulier, Steve Sherman

Jacket Blurb: Steve Sherman, John Vance

Management: John Vance, Koen Vyverman